THE GUNSMITH

482

The Chanteuse from the East

Books by J.R. Roberts
(Robert J. Randisi)

The Gunsmith series

Gunsmith Giant series

Lady Gunsmith series

Angel Eyes series

Tracker series

Mountain Jack Pike series

COMING SOON!
The Gunsmith
483 – Belle Starr's Daughter

THE GUNSMITH

482

The Chanteuse from the East

J.R. Roberts

SPEAKING VOLUMES, LLC
NAPLES, FLORIDA
2023

The Chanteuse from the East

ISBN 978-1-64540-953-3

Chapter One

Chanteuse Clarice DuPont burst angrily into her dressing room, backstage at the Metropolitan Theater, startling her manager. He leaped out of his seat as the door slammed into the wall.

"What the hell—" he cried.

"He was out there again tonight!" she snapped.

"What? Where?"

"First damn row!" she screamed at him. She tore her gown off, leaving one of her perfect, large breasts completely bare. Luckily, that sort of nudity did not appeal to her agent, which was one of the reasons she had originally hired him. She often needed her manager in her dressing room when dressing. This man, Leo Delaware, was the only man she had ever employed who did not stare. His preferences ran elsewhere.

"You told me you were going to keep him out," she went on, "that you were going to keep me safe."

"I'm sorry, Clarice," Delaware said. "I don't know how he got in, but I have an idea."

"What now?" She put her hands on her hips and glared at him, still half topless.

"Sit down," he said. "Take a breath."

She took a deep breath, grabbed a robe and slipped it on, then sat in front of her mirror.

"What is it?" she asked.

"I want you to go on tour."

"On tour where?" she asked. "We've played all the main venues up and down the east coast."

"I know," he said. "I'm talking about going west."

"Where, exactly?" she asked, frowning.

"I thought we'd start in Pittsburgh, then just keep moving west to Chicago, St. Louis, Kansas City, and then across the Mississippi."

Her eyes widened.

"You want me to go to the Wild West?"

"It's not so wild anymore, Clarice," he argued. "It's a lot more civilized than it used to be. And going west would get you away from this nut that's following you."

"And what makes you think we won't encounter more nuts along the way?"

"I thought of that," he said. "I'm going to get you a bodyguard."

"A bodyguard?" she asked. "Like who? "Do you think you're going to find someone from New York who can handle gunfighters and savages?"

"No, not from New York," Delaware said. "I thought since we're going west, we should hire someone from there."

"And how would you know who to hire?" she demanded. "We might end up with some ruffian who would rob us and kill us."

"Do you remember when we played D.C.?"

"What's that got to do with touring the west?"

"I've discussed the situation with some people we met there. Do you remember a man named Artemus Gordon?"

"I do," she said. "A very charming man who works for the government."

"He works for the president," Delaware said. "And he knows a man who would be perfect for this assignment."

"Assignment?" she asked. "Being my bodyguard is an assignment?"

"Gordon was here in New York. We had dinner and discussed the entire situation. He even offered to find out who's following you. But when I told him we wanted to go west, he said he knew just the man."

"Who?"

"Fellow named Clint Adams," Delaware said.

She frowned.

"Why do I know that name?"

Delaware took a rolled-up dime novel from his pocket and handed it to her.

"Oh, the Gunsmith." She stared at him. "But he's a gunfighter."

"Gordon says he can handle a gun better than anyone he ever saw, but that doesn't make him a gunfighter."

"What does it make him?" she asked.

"According to Gordon, it makes him the man for the job," Delaware said.

"Do you really think he'll do it?" she asked.

"Well," Delaware said, "he's also supposed to be something of a lady's man."

"Do you expect me to flirt with him?"

"Not at all," Delaware said. "I don't really think you'd have to."

Clarice looked at herself in the mirror, caressed her bare breast in one hand and said, "Probably not."

Chapter Two

Delaware and Clarice met Artemus Gordon at the Metropole for dinner to discuss the tour. The Maître d' showed the songstress and her manager to the table where Gordon was already seated.

"Miss DuPont," Gordon said, "nice to see you again."

He took her hand and almost kissed it, then shook hands with Delaware. The greetings complete, he sat across from Clarice.

"Thank you for meeting with us, Mr. Gordon," Delaware said.

"My pleasure," Gordon said. "I enjoyed tonight's performance as much as I did last month in Washington."

"Oh, you were there," Clarice said. "I wish you had come backstage."

"I knew we'd be having dinner tonight," Gordon said.

They took the time to peruse the Metropole's excellent menu, and then ordered, adding two bottles of wine, one white and one red.

"I presume you had a reason for this meeting," Gordon said.

"Yes," Delaware said, "you and I spoke shortly last month about a tour we are planning, to go west."

"Yes," Gordon said, "I remember. You wanted a recommendation for a bodyguard."

"That's right, and you mentioned a friend of yours, Clint Adams."

"To be precise," Gordon said, "Mr. Adams is friends with my partner, Jim West. But yes, he and I are acquainted and have worked together."

"Do you think he'd be interested in this job?" Delaware asked.

"Clint doesn't really take jobs," Gordon said.

"What would you call it, then?" Clarice asked.

"He does favors," Gordon said, "and he does things he thinks will interest him."

"So do you think this will interest him?" she asked.

"It's not something I can recall he's done before, so it's possible."

"How would we go about this?" Delaware asked. "Do we approach him ourselves?"

"Or would you consent to do it for us?" Clarice added.

"I suspect the best way to go would be for me to ask him to meet with you," Gordon said, "and then you could make your request."

"So you suggest we put it in the form of a request, and not a job?" Clarice said.

"Exactly," Gordon said.

"What sort of things have you and he worked on in the past?" Clarice asked.

"Certain government jobs that I can't really discuss," Gordon said.

"I see Clarice said."

The waiter appeared with their plates and set the two bottles of wine down on the table.

"Where would we find him?" Delaware asked.

"I'd have to send some telegrams to locate him and then set up a meeting."

"Here, in New York?" Delaware asked.

"That remains to be seen," Gordon said. "We'll have to see where he is."

"How likely do you think it is he would come here?" Clarice asked.

"Highly unlikely," Gordon said, "unless we find him already nearby."

"How soon do you think you could arrange this?" Clarice asked.

"I can send the telegrams tomorrow."

"We would like to leave New York as soon as possible," Delaware said.

"Then I'll send the telegrams first thing in the morning."

"How soon would you expect a reply?" Clarice asked.

"That would depend on when I locate him," Gordon explained. "I suspect he would reply almost immediately."

"All right," Delaware said, "why don't we enjoy our dinner?"

***

After dinner and dessert, Gordon said he had to leave.

"I'm sorry, but I have another meeting," he told them. "I'll contact you at your hotel tomorrow after I've sent some telegrams. Where are you staying?"

"We're at the Waldorf," Delaware said.

"Until tomorrow, then. Thank you for dinner."

"Thank you for meeting with us," Clarice said.

Gordon left, then Clarice and Delaware each ordered a drink.

"So what do you think?" Clarice asked.

"I think we're going to get him."

“He said they weren’t friends,” Clarice pointed out.

“They’ve worked together, that should be enough.”

“Worked together on what, I wonder. Have we ever heard what Mr. Gordon’s position is?”

“It’s in the government,” Delaware said. “That’s all we need to know.”

“Do you think we should have told him about our fan?”

“Why muddle things?” Delaware answered, sitting back in his chair. “We’ll only tell him what he needs to know.”

Chapter Three

As luck would have it, Clint Adams was in Boston having just concluded a visit in Hannibal Missouri with his friend, Sam Clemens, otherwise known as Mark Twain.

He had let his friend, John Locke, who had a ranch in Las Vegas, New Mexico, know where he would be, so when Locke got the telegram from New York, he relayed the message to Clint.

When the desk clerk handed Clint the telegram, he read it immediately. Locke and Clint had reacted so quickly that it was literally two days later when Clint sent Artemus Gordon a telegram in New York. Since Clint had already been considering a stop in New York before heading back west, he agreed to meet with Miss Clarice DuPont and her manager. It was also fortunate that Clint had heard of the singer, although had never seen any of her performances. Up to this point she had only performed in the East.

***

After reading the telegram and having breakfast, Artemus Gordon went to the Waldorf Astoria Hotel and asked for Leo Delaware's room number. The desk clerk had been advised that he should be given the number when he arrived. The room was on the second floor, so Gordon was able to avoid the elevator and take the stairs. He knocked on Delaware's door and the man answered promptly.

"Come in," he told Gordon "Coffee?"

"No, thank you. I just had breakfast. I'm on my way to catch a train, but I wanted to let you know I heard from Clint Adams. He's actually in Boston and is taking a train down here to meet with you and Clarice."

"That's fabulous!" Delaware exclaimed. "When?"

"He should be here tomorrow," Gordon said. "He'll come to see you right here."

"I'll let the desk know to let him in," Delaware said, "I can't thank you enough, Mr. Gordon."

"You should know that he's coming to meet the two of you, he hasn't yet agreed to travel with you. You'll have to convince him."

"I'll leave that up to Clarice," Delaware told him. "She can be very persuasive."

The two men shook hands and Gordon left to catch his train.

As soon as Gordon was gone, Delaware left his room to go to Clarice's suite. He knocked and she answered immediately. She was radiantly beautiful in a purple, silk gown.

"Adams will be here tomorrow," he told her, walking past her to enter the suite.

She closed the door and turned to face him.

"He's agreed?"

"Not yet," Delaware said. "He happens to be in Boston, so he's taking the train down to meet with us. It's going to be up to you, darling, to convince him."

"And I'll do it," she said. "Right now, I'd like breakfast in my room."

"I'll take care of it," he said. "Meanwhile, you figure out what tactic you'll take with the Gunsmith."

He left the room, leaving her alone to plan . . .

***

Clint Adams agreed to the meeting for two reasons. he had heard of Clarice—the Chanteuse of the East—and Clint was close friends with Jim West. Gordon was not only West's partner, but his close friend, as well. And even if he went to New York and did not agree to whatever their request was, he looked forward to meeting the woman. It was said she not only sang like an angel but looked like one as well.

He secured a ticket on the train for New York.

***

Delaware left Clarice's suite and went downstairs to the dining room to personally get the songstress' breakfast. Clarice liked her eggs a certain way, and Delaware made sure she always got what she wanted. And to do that, he always went right to the kitchen.

He had done this several times now, but never before had the kitchen been empty when he entered.

"Is anybody here?" he called out.

He heard a muffled sound and started walking around the large kitchen. When he spotted one of the chefs on the floor, hogtied hands and feet, and gagged, he started toward him. He took two steps before someone came up behind him and wrapped a thick arm around his throat. The hold, if applied long enough, would have killed him, but the attacker also had one of the kitchen's knives in his hand. He was tall enough to drag Delaware up onto his toes, and then drive the knife into his back.

Two men entered the kitchen, saw what was happening and yelled. But they were chefs and not brave enough to charge the man and grab him. Startled, the killer dropped the knife, glared at the two chefs, and then calmly walked from the kitchen.

Delaware's body was left on the floor, in a pool of blood.

Chapter Four

When Clint entered the Waldorf lobby the next day, he immediately knew that something was wrong. There were uniformed members of the New York City Police Department at every door. He was watched closely as he approached the front desk. The clerk was an experienced looking individual in his thirties.

"Can I help you, sir?" the desk clerk asked.

"What's going on?" Clint asked.

"There's was some . . . trouble last night," the man replied.

Clint looked around again and saw that all the officers were eyeing him.

"I'm here to see Mr. Leo Delaware, or Miss Clarice DuPont."

"Oh," the man said, suddenly becoming nervous, "yes." It looked to Clint like the man gave some sort of signal. Suddenly the police were closing in on him. Usually when he visited Manhattan, Clint wore a jacket that would cover his sidearm, or a shoulder rig for his New Line. Today, he had his holster on beneath the jacket. Because the uniformed officers looked so intense, he made sure to keep his hands away from his side.

In the midst of the office was another man, this one wearing a simple suit. He was older than the others, and not quite as intense looking.

"Sir?" he said. "Would you stand very still for a moment, please?"

"I am standing still," Clint pointed out, "and my hands are away from my gun."

"I see that," the man said. "My name is Inspector Meade of the New York City Police. Do you mind if I take your gun?"

"I mind very much," Clint said, "but it seems I have little choice."

Meade plucked Clint's gun from his holster and stuck it in his own belt.

"Now would you mind telling me your name?"

"Clint Adams."

"And Mr. Adams, you're here to see . . ."

"Mr. Delaware and Miss DuPont."

"And what's your business with them?"

"None, right now," Clint said. "I'm simply here to meet them."

"I'm sorry, sir," the forty-something Inspector said, "it's just occurred to me . . . are you Clint Adams, the Gunsmith?"

"Yes."

The officers virtually surrounding them all became tense.

"Mr. Adams, I'm going to need something a little more informative from you."

"I was asked by a good friend to come to New York and meet with Mr. Delaware and Miss DuPont," Clint explained.

"For what purpose?" Meade asked.

"Apparently, they have a . . . favor to ask of me. I was in Boston, and since I know who Miss DuPont is, I agreed to come down and meet with them. I arrived this morning and, as you can see from my suitcase, I haven't even gotten myself a hotel room, yet. I chose to meet with Miss DuPont, first. Now perhaps you'd tell me what this is all about?"

"Yes, of course," Meade said. "Mr. Delaware was killed yesterday morning, knifed in the back." He took Clint's gun from his belt and handed it back. "I assume you feel undressed without this?"

"You assume correctly." Clint took the gun and holstered it. "How's Miss DuPont?"

"As I'm sure you'd assume, she's very upset. Apparently, Mr. Delaware was not only her manager, but her very good friend."

"Is there any reason I can't see her?"

"Not at all," Meade said, "but I hope there's no reason why I can't come along?"

"Be my guest," Clint said.

"Then I'll show you to her suite." He turned and gestured to the clerk. "Would you hold Mr. Adams' suitcase for him, please?"

"Of course, sir," the clerk said, accepting it as Clint handed it over the desk.

"This way, please," Meade said.

"Would you mind if we use the stairs?" Clint asked. "I'm not fond of elevators."

"Not at all," Meade said, "I don't much like them, myself," and led the way.

***

When they reached the door of Clarice DuPont's suite Inspector Meade knocked. The door was opened by a woman whose beauty was only dulled by the sadness in her eyes.

"Miss DuPont," the policeman said, "I'm Inspector Meade of the—"

"Yes, I remember, Inspector."

"This is Clint Adams," Meade said. "He says he has an appointment with you."

"Yes, of course he does," Clarice said, backing away. "Please, come in."

Clint and Meade both entered. Clarice closed the door and turned to face them.

Chapter Five

"I'm sorry we have to meet under such circumstances," Clint said.

"It's horrible," she said, "horrible."

"Why don't we sit?" Clint asked.

He took her elbow and led her to a sofa.

"The Inspector would like to sit in on this meeting, if you don't mind?" Clint asked.

"Not at all. Leo meant this to be a lunch, but . . ."

"I understand."

She sat, and he lowered himself into an adjacent armchair. The Inspector remained standing.

"Mr. Gordon didn't give me many facts," Clint said, "but I assume things have changed in light of what's happened."

"Not at all," Clarice said. "I intend to go ahead with our plans, especially in light of what I discovered in Leo's room."

"Which was what?"

"We were going to tour theaters throughout the West," she replied. "I found that he had already planned the tour and had it all down in writing. All of the theaters are already booked."

"But without your manager—" Clint started.

"I'm perfectly able to conduct my own tour, Mr. Adams," she cut in. "Leo and I had been together a long time. I know every aspect of the business."

"So you intend to go on this tour?"

"I do."

"And what was the reason you wanted to meet with me?" he asked.

"Leo believed I needed a bodyguard for the trip."

"And why's that?"

"We've been here in Manhattan for a week—two performances—and the same man has been at each one."

"Doing what?" Clint asked.

"Sitting in front, glaring at me."

"And?"

"That's it," she said. "Glaring at me as if he wanted to . . . to kill me."

"Well," Clint said, scratching his head, "in light of what's happened I guess I can't say you were imagining things. But he never made a move? Sent a note? Tried to get to your dressing room?"

"No," she said. "He just glared."

"Why was that an issue, Miss DuPont?" the Inspector asked, speaking for the first time.

"Inspector," she said, "I hope you won't think me unduly full of myself when I say that men don't usually glare at me."

"I imagine not," he said. "You're a beautiful woman."

"I wondered why this man would buy a front row ticket—twice—if that was all he wanted to do."

"Can you describe this man, Miss DuPont."

"Yes, he was—"

"Not right now," he said. "After you've finished your business with Mr. Adams, I'll have one of my men take it down."

"All right."

"So you want to hire me as a bodyguard?" Clint asked.

"Mr. Gordon made it clear you probably would not take this as a paying job," she said. "Leo and I were hoping you would come along as an escort. Perhaps your presence would . . . dissuade anyone from following."

"But that logic was before what happened last night," he pointed out.

"Yes, it was."

"What are you thinking now?" he asked.

She put her right hand to her forehead.

"I don't know," she said, "I don't want to offend you by offering you a job, like a common . . . bodyguard."

"I think a common bodyguard might be just what you need," Clint said. "What do you think, Inspector?"

"On one hand I would suggest canceling the entire tour, but on the other hand I'd suggest getting out of Manhattan until I can find this killer." He looked at Clarice. "I'm sorry if that's no help."

"Naturally, I want you to find this killer, and if staying here would help you do that, I'll stay."

"I think staying here would put you in danger," Meade said. "But going on the tour might do the same." He looked sheepish. "Again, not much help."

"Then I intend to go on the tour."

"Then I agree with Mr. Adams. You need a bodyguard."

Clarice looked at Clint.

"Can you recommend someone?"

"Of course I can," he answered, "but you haven't offered me the job, yet."

"But I thought—"

"I have acted as a bodyguard before, usually for a high-ranking government official."

"I thought they had secret service for that," Meade said.

"When my government calls on me for help, I answer," Clint said.

"But you are certainly no common bodyguard," she said. "And I've insulted you, already."

"I've been insulted many times before. I think I'll survive."

"Then you'll do it?"

"I should at least make sure you leave Manhattan safely," he said. "After that we can discuss what else I can do, or who I can recommend. "Is that fair?"

"Very fair," she said, "but we have to agree on payment—" she went on, but Clint stopped her.

"All you have to do is foot the bills for travel, meals and boarding. Again, anything else we can discuss later."

"That sounds very fair," she said.

"I think," the Inspector added, "you might start by getting Mr. Adams a room for the rest of your stay here."

"We're scheduled to depart in two days," she said.

"Good," Clint said, "that'll give me time to take a bath, and look over your travel itinerary."

"I must say," Clarice said, walking the two men to the door, "you certainly don't sound like a common bodyguard."

"I have an idea, Miss DuPont," he said, "let's stop using the word 'common.' "

"Agreed," she said, "if you'll call me Clarice."

"And I'm Clint."

"Would you please come back to my suite tonight for dinner, Clint?"

"It'd be my pleasure. And I'm sure the Inspector will have some men watching out for you the rest of your stay here."

"Yes, indeed," Meade said. "I'll have men on every door, as well as watching this hall. And I'll return with a man who will take down the description of this glaring fellow so we can watch for him."

"I want to thank you, gentlemen," she said, as she opened the door. "I feel safer already."

Chapter Six

Clint was given what was probably the smallest room the Waldorf had, but it was still better than most other rooms he had ever stayed in. It overlooked the front of the hotel, but it was on a high enough floor that there was no access from outside.

The room had indoor plumbing, so a bath was an easy thing to have and enjoy. And since he was going to have dinner with a beautiful woman, he made use of a service the hotel had to have his clothing and boots cleaned. Clarice had a bellboy deliver the paperwork regarding her tour to Clint's room, and he studied them while reclining in the large, porcelain tub. By the time he was ready to dress, he had the tour imprinted on his mind. There were major stops in Pittsburgh, Chicago, St. Louis, Kansas City, and smaller ones in Abilene, Oklahoma City, and Tombstone's Birdcage Theater.

He dressed in his newly cleaned clothes, donned the jacket to hide his Colt New Line in his shoulder holster, and then pulled on his newly cleaned boots. These were not the boots he would wear when he rode his Tobiano, Toby, who he had left with John Locke on his Las Vegas ranch. Locke was a rancher who raised horses, but was also known as The Widowmaker from his early life as a gunman. Now he only took jobs to support his ranch. Clint was wondering about recommending Locke as Clarice DuPont's bodyguard.

He left his room and walked up the stairs to Clarice DuPont's suite. When she opened the door, she was wearing a powder blue gown that showed her arms but covered her cleavage, which he could see would have been impressive.

"Good-evening, Clint," she said "Come in."

As he walked past her, he caught her scent, which was heady.

"You look beautiful," he said.

"You look rather dashing, yourself," she said, closing the door. "I was considering dressing down because of what happened to Leo, but I decided he wouldn't have wanted me to wallow. It was Leo who told me to try and always look my best. So this is for him." She touched her auburn hair, which was hanging down to her shoulders. "I couldn't do much with my hair."

"It looks great," he assured her.

"Thank you. Dinner should be here shortly," she said. "They're going to bring it up in the elevator and wheel it in here on a table with wheels. The Waldorf has all the modern conveniences."

"I know," he said, "I took advantage of some of them, myself."

"I had some wine brought up earlier. It's chilling. Would you like some now?"

"I can wait for dinner to arrive."

"Then we can sit and talk while we wait."

This time they both sat on the sofa instead of him sitting across from her.

"Have you had time to look over the tour schedule?" she asked.

"I have," he said. "It's impressive, but it includes some touchy locations."

"The kind where I would need a bodyguard, anyway, even if there wasn't a crazy man out there?"

"Yes," Clint said, "sometimes the most dangerous men out there are the ones liquored up and having a good time. Not the crazy ones."

"Places like where?"

"Well, Tombstone, for one," Clint said. "Wyatt Earp used to deal Faro at the Birdcage, and now 'the Chanteuse from the East' will be playing there."

She shook her head.

"That name was Leo's idea," she said.

"Well, when I got Gordon's telegram, I remembered it."

"So you heard of me before that? Had you ever heard me sing?"

"Yes, I heard of you, but no, never heard you sing. I suppose the first stop in Pittsburgh will be my chance."

There was a knock at the door at that point, and Clint held a hand out to keep her seated.

"I'll get it," he said.

He rose, walked to the door and opened it carefully. There was a bellboy with a cart on wheels laden with covered plates.

"Dinner, sir," the boy said.

"Show me," Clint said, pointing to the plates.

"Yes, sir."

He removed one cover at a time, revealing plates with thick steaks covered with onions and surrounded by vegetables, and enough salad and rolls for four people. There were also two glasses and a bottle of champagne.

"Wait a minute," he told the boy.

Clint examined the top more closely, then lifted the white cloth that hung down the sides, to look underneath.

"Wheel it in," Clint said.

"Yes, sir."

The boy pushed the cart in and stopped when Clint said, "That's good." He tipped the boy and said, "Thank you very much,"

"Thank *you,* sir."

As the boy left, Clarice stood up and walked to the cart. She removed one cloche and stared at the thick, juicy steak.

"It looks wonderful," she said, setting the cover down and removing another one.

"The Waldorf is supposed to have a very good kitchen," he commented.

"This isn't from their kitchen," she said. "I had them bring it in from outside. I don't want to eat anything prepared in the kitchen where Leo was killed."

Clint nodded his understanding.

"Of course."

"Shall we eat?" she asked.

Clint walked across the room to fetch two chairs and bring them to the cart, which expanded into almost a full-sized table. He held her chair for her, then sat across from her, and indicated their glasses.

"Champagne?" he asked.

"Please," she said.

He took the bottle from the ice bucket, popped the cork and poured. When he sat, she lifted the glass for a toast, and he grabbed his.

"To Leo," she said.

He lifted his glass, nodded and they sipped. Then they started eating . . .

Chapter Seven

They got into the meal, making small talk all the while. When they were finished, Clarice sat back and said, “I hope you don’t mind, I didn’t order any dessert. That was always Leo’s favorite part of the meal. It didn’t seem right having it without him.”

“I understand.” There was a coffee pot and two cups on the table. “Coffee?” he asked.

“Yes, please.”

He filled both cups.

“What were you doing in Boston, if you don’t mind my asking.”

“My friend Sam Clemens was there as part of the lecture tour.”

“You’re friends with Mark Twain?” she asked in surprise.

“For a long time.”

“And you came all the way east to hear him?”

“He was stopping there before touring Europe,” Clint said. “I wanted to see him off.”

“You must have an interesting collection of friends,” she said.

"I have an interesting collection of acquaintances," he said, "and a few good friends. Sam is one of the friends."

"And Mr. Gordon?"

"More of an acquaintance, but his partner, Jim West, is a good friend."

"And do you have a woman waiting for you back west?" she asked.

"No," he said, "I'm unattached."

"No family?"

He decided not to go into his history, which began in the East and took him West.

"No family," he said. "What about you?"

"Leo was my family," she said." He was like my brother."

"And no romantic attachments?"

"There have been men," she admitted, "but no attachments. I suppose you believe a woman my age should be married and have children."

He guessed her to be in her early thirties, although she certainly could have passed for younger.

"That's up to you," he said. "I believe we should all live our own lives and not bend to what society expects of us."

"So you're never getting married? Having children?"

"I think that time has passed for me," Clint said.

"I've seen some of the dime novels about you," she said. "Are they not true?"

"Exaggerations," he told her. "They'd have people think I came out of the womb with a gun in each hand."

She laughed and asked, "Not true?"

He held up a forefinger and said, "One gun."

She laughed again, then her expression grew grave.

"I don't think it's right that I'm laughing," she said. "Not with poor Leo . . ." She trailed off and tears began to fall.

"Will there be a funeral?" he asked.

"Oh, no," she said. "There was only Leo and me. "I'm having his body shipped back to Maine, where we come from. That's where he would have wanted to be buried."

"You're not going with it?"

"He'd want me to go on this tour," she said. "When it's over I'll go back home and grieve. Do you think that's . . . cold?"

"As I told you, people should make their own decisions. It doesn't matter what others think."

"I'm interested in what you think."

"I think we all grieve in our own way," he said. "You seem to know what Leo would have wanted. He wouldn't have wanted his death to change that."

"He certainly wouldn't have wanted the actions of a mad man to change our plans," she said, wiping her tears away with her napkin.

Clint took his napkin from his lap and dropped it on top of his empty plate.

"I'll leave you to rest," he said.

"Of course," she said rising. "You undoubtedly need some rest, as well, before we start." They walked to the door together. "Can we have dinner again tomorrow night? Perhaps we can go out."

"Dinner, definitely," Clint said, "but if there is a madman out there, why take the chance?"

"Of course, you're right."

"If you'd like to get out of the hotel—"

"No, no," she said, "you're right, of course."

"All your performances in New York are done?" he asked.

"Oh yes," she said, "I had two performances scheduled, and fulfilled them."

"I suppose you'll have a lot of free time tomorrow."

"Oh, I have to pack for the tour," she said. "You know how women are about packing. And I have other ways to pass my time. I'm sure the Inspector will want to talk to me again before I leave."

"Did you give his man a description of the glaring man?" Clint asked.

"Oh yes," Clarice said. "He assured me they'd be out combing the streets for him."

"I'll say good night, then," he said. "I'll push this cart out into the hall and have a bellman collect it."

"Very well."

She opened the door for him and he took her hand.

"Don't open this door for anyone but me," he instructed.

"What about the Inspector?"

"You'll recognize his voice."

"Oh, yes."

"Very well," he said, "but no one else. If I'm going to be your escort and bodyguard, you'll have to do everything I tell you to do."

"Yes, sir," she said. "I hear and obey."

Clint wheeled the cart out, listened for her to lock her door, then returned to his own room.

Chapter Eight

Before getting back to his room Clint decided to go down and see who was in the lobby. As he reached the area, he saw several uniformed police officers spread about. They all acknowledged him as he walked past to the front desk. The desk clerk there was a different, younger one, but Clint could see that he recognized him.

"Mr. Adams," the young man said, "what can I do for you?"

"Is the Inspector still in the hotel?"

"No, sir," the clerk said, "he went to his headquarters."

"Did he say when he'd be returning?"

"Yes, sir," the clerk answered, "he said he'd be back in the morning, to see that the Chanteuse remains safe until she's ready to go."

"I see."

"Is that all right?"

"That's just fine," Clint said. "Thank you."

He assumed that meant Meade and some of his men would also escort them to the train the following day. Clint decided that, from this day on, the job of keeping

Clarice safe was his. Once they were on the train going west, he would decide how to further proceed.

He turned and went back to his room.

***

The man who murdered Leo Delaware watched as Clint Adams went up the stairs. He looked around at the uniformed men in the lobby and knew he was safe as long as he remained where he was. But there was no way he could get to Clarice DuPont's suite, or to the songstress herself. Not while the police—and Clint Adams—were around. If Adams went with the woman, he would have to deal with them during the tour.

But at least he had managed to dispose of that flamboyant manager of hers.

He left the Waldorf for the night to report to his boss and find out the next move for tomorrow.

***

When Clint left the suite Clarice undressed, donned her robe, then curled up in bed and cried. She had to continue on without Leo, and hopefully Clint Adams would agree to stay with her for the entire tour. So far she trusted him, and felt safe with him, even though they had only just met. She hoped nothing would happen to change that.

***

The next morning Clint knew he could have left the Waldorf and found plenty of good places for breakfast up and down Lexington Avenue, or on some of the side streets, but he wanted to stay inside the hotel in case Clarice went looking for him.

He was recognized as soon as he walked in and shown to an isolated table which was specifically for people who didn't want to be disturbed. There were other guests dining there, but he couldn't hear any of their conversations, which suited him.

He ordered a monstrous breakfast which included flapjacks, eggs, rashers of bacon, fried potatoes, and biscuits. He was also offered waffles but turned them down. As he was eating, the waiter came to him and said, "Inspector Meade would like to join you, sir."

"By all means."

The waiter led the Inspector over and the man seemed glassy-eyed as he looked at Clint's breakfast.

"Have you had breakfast yet, Inspector?" Clint asked, as the man sat across from him.

"Uh, actually, no, but—"

"Bring the Inspector everything I have, and another pot of coffee."

"Yes, sir."

Clint poured the last of the first pot into a cup for the policeman.

"You'll enjoy this breakfast," Clint said. "It's excellent."

"I have to admit" Meade said, "I've never been here before. It's a little out of my budget."

"Don't worry," Clint said, "it'll all be taken care of by Miss DuPont."

When the feast was laid out in front of Meade, Clint suggested the man eat before they started talking. That suited the Inspector just fine.

Chapter Nine

Over a third pot of coffee, the two men talked.

"I've circulated the description of the man Miss DuPont saw at her performances in Carnegie Hall."

Clint had heard of Carnegie Hall, and seen it from the outside, but had never been inside.

"That's an amazing structure," he commented.

"And she filled it, both times."

"Did you see her performance?"

"I'm afraid not," Meade said. "Also beyond my budget, like this breakfast. I don't know how I'll be able to eat a normal breakfast after this. In any case, if this fellow is walking the streets, we'll find him."

"I doubt he'll be out in the open," Clint said. "I just don't want him to be at the train station when Miss DuPont is there."

"Don't worry," Meade said, "you'll have an escort to the station. You'll get underway safely."

"That's good."

"How is the lady doing?"

"She's remarkable," Clint said. "She'll be remaining in her suite until we leave. I had dinner with her there last night and will again tonight. But she's having the food brought in from outside. She doesn't want any food cooked in the kitchen where her manager was killed."

"I don't blame her," Meade said. "Were she and the gentleman, uh, romantically involved?"

"She said they were like brother and sister."

"In some ways, that's worse."

"She almost broke down in front of me last night but regained her composure. I'm sure she's doing her grieving in private."

"She's entitled," Meade said.

"What's on your mind?" Clint asked. "Are you here to talk with me, again?"

"Actually," Meade said, "I thought perhaps Miss DuPont might have thought of something else she could tell me about this man who was glaring at her."

"Why don't we go upstairs and ask her?" Clint suggested.

They left the dining room and went up to Clarice's suite. They saw her breakfast tray out in the hall, an indication that she still had her appetite. Clint knocked on the door, and it was opened by Clarice, once again wearing that silk robe.

"Gentlemen," she said, "How nice." She touched her hair. "Please excuse the way I look."

"I'm afraid the blame for this is mine, Miss DuPont, not Mr. Adams'. I just wanted to ask a few more questions."

"Of course, Inspector," she said. "I'm available to help all I can."

She allowed them to enter and closed the door.

"I'm afraid I can't offer you anything," she said. "I just finished my breakfast."

"As did we," Meade said.

"Then I suppose you might as well ask your questions."

They all sat. Meade actually rehashed the entire story, then asked Clarice if she remembered anything else about the glaring man.

"I'm afraid not," she said. "I've told you all I know."

"All right, then," he said, standing. "I'll get back to it."

He and Clint stood.

"Clint, can you stay a moment?"

"Of course."

Clint walked Meade to the door.

"I'll see you both in the morning to escort you safely to your train."

"Thank you, Inspector," Clarice said.

"Thanks for breakfast," Meade said to Clint, and left.

Chapter Ten

After Inspector Meade left, Clint returned to the sofa to sit with Clarice.

"I just wanted to go over the travel plans Leo had set up," she said.

"Of course," Clint said, "whatever he arranged is fine with me."

"I have a sleeping car whenever we travel by train, and Leo always sat in the passenger car."

"No problem," Clint said. "You're the one who needs to be rested."

"And if there's a dining car," she went on, "I'll eat in private. And you can join me when you like."

"I'll want to keep an eye on the passengers," Clint said, "but I don't see any reason why we wouldn't be able to dine together."

"Do you think someone will try something on the train?" she asked.

"After an attack in the kitchen, who knows? Clint asked. "I just want to keep you safe."

"I suppose I should be glad you're thinking that way."

"Tell me," Clint said, "is there any chance the killer was after Leo the whole time? And not you?"

"I don't see why," she said. "And that man was glaring at me the whole time."

"If the glaring man was the killer, at all," Clint observed.

"So maybe there was that man and a killer?" she asked. "Now I'm really confused."

"Maybe before we leave New York you should rethink this whole thing. You might decide you want to go back home to Maine."

"There's nothing for me there," she said. "Leo and I left Maine a long time ago. No, I'm doing this tour." She stood up. "I better get started packing. You should, too."

"I've only got the one bag," he said.

"You men are so lucky," she said, as they walked to the door. "You don't have all the bother that women do."

She opened the door, and he stepped out.

"I'll see you tonight for dinner," he said.

"I'm going to dress a bit more casual tonight, if that's all right with you."

"I'm sure you'll look beautiful no matter what you wear. Would you like me to arrange the meal tonight?"

"I've already spoken with the concierge about bringing it in from outside again."

"See you tonight, then."

"Once again, he waited until she had locked the door, then walked down the hall.

***

Clint had a book of Mark Twain's short stories with him. He enjoyed rereading 'The Celebrated Jumping Frog of Calaveras County' every so oft, so he started with that.

Clint had several friends in New York, including two men he used for backup when needed: Jacoby, who lived in Manhattan, and another named Delvecchio, who resided in Brooklyn. But he wasn't going to be in the city long enough to contact both of them.

He finished the story and put the book aside rather than continue on. He decided to go down to the hotel's bar, The Bull & Bear, and have a beer or two.

Downstairs, he walked across the lobby to enter the Bull & Bear from there. The place mainly catered to guests of the hotel, so it wasn't crowded.

He walked to the bar, where he was greeted by a bartender wearing a black vest over a long-sleeved white shirt. He was tall and fit, in his thirties.

"What can I get you Mr. Adams?" he asked.

"Does everyone in the hotel know who I am?"

"We always keep track of our famous and important guests." The man said.

"Well, I don't know which one I am right now, but I'll have a beer."

"Yes, sir."

The bartender put a frosty mug of beer down on the bar in front of Clint, who picked it up and gulped from it, gratefully.

"How is it?" the barman asked.

"Very good," Clint said. "Thanks."

"No problem," the bartender said, wiping the bar. "There's not much to do this time of day."

"When do you get busy?"

"Well, we serve food, right about meal times, especially dinner. Have you had our steak?"

"No," Clint said, "last night the lady and I had steaks from outside."

"That have something to do with that killing the other night?"

"It does."

"Can't say I blame her," the barman said. "That's not the kind of blood you want with your steak. 'scuse me."

He walked to the other end of the bar to serve another customer.

Chapter Eleven

Clint dressed, hoping he wasn't too casual, and walked to Clarice's suite. When he knocked on the door, she answered wearing her silk robe, her hair pinned up, tendrils hanging down.

As he entered she said, "I just wanted to get my hair out of my eyes. I hope it's okay."

"It's fine."

"Dinner just got here, so it should still be hot."

"Good."

The table was all set up, and he saw that they both had large bowls of stew, there was a basket of bread in the center.

"I hope this is okay," she said. "It's nothing fancy."

"It looks good."

They both sat.

"Just water today, no wine," she said. "I noticed you weren't very fond of it last night."

"I prefer beer."

"I'll remember that as we travel," she said.

They each went at their stew with forks, as there were large chunks of meat in it. When the meat was gone, they switched to spoons and used them for whatever they couldn't soak up with the bread.

When the meal was finished, Clint wheeled the cart into the hallway. They then sat on the sofa together.

"What did you do today while I packed?" she asked.

"I read some Twain, packed, went downstairs, had a look around and a couple of beers."

"Did you see anyone?"

"Just the men Inspector Meade left here," Clint said. "I saw some other guests in the lobby and the bar, but none who looked like your glaring man."

"If he's on the train with us, I'll recognize him."

"If you see him, I'll take care of him. But first we want to find out if he killed your manager."

"I agree we should do that."

"I have a question."

"What's that?"

"Don't you travel with musicians?"

"Leo always books—booked—me into theaters that were outfitted with musicians. Then we would arrive early enough to rehearse with them."

"And what if the musicians aren't up to your standards?" Clint asked.

"Then we cancel."

"That's taking a big chance."

"If a theater is willing to pay me, they will provide the musicians."

"And you're willing to travel across the West on that promise?"

"I am," she said. "I should say, we were, Leo and I, but now it's me."

"And me."

"Why?" she asked. "You hardly know me."

"You've suffered a great loss," Clint said, "and you're not letting it destroy you."

"Leo would be ashamed of me if I did that."

"Someone with that much courage deserves the chance to complete her plan. Besides, I'd be heading back West, anyway."

"So we'll part company at some point," she said, "when you get to where you want to go."

"Yes."

"And where will that be?"

"I don't know," Clint said. "My horse is in Las Vegas, New Mexico. You have a performance planned for Albuquerque. They're a hundred miles apart. We'll see what happens when we get that far."

"That sounds good."

"I suppose I'd better give you some time to rest," Clint said, starting to rise.

"No, wait . . ." Clarice snapped.

He turned to look at her.

"What's wrong?"

"I've been resting all day," she said, taking his hands and tugging him back toward the sofa.

"I thought you spent the day packing?"

"Well, yes, but other than that," she said. "Let's sit and talk. We're going to be together for a long time, even if you're not with me for the entire tour. Let's take some time and get to know each other."

"I think we've gotten to know each other pretty well over dinner, these last two nights," Clint commented.

"I don't mean that," she said, squeezing his hands. "I want something else."

"What's that?"

"Something that will help me stop thinking," she said. "I don't want to think anymore."

She released his hands and stepped back. As he watched she untied the silk robe and let it fall to the floor. He had been able to see that she was naked underneath, the way the silk stuck to her skin. The outline of her nipples beneath the fabric made it very clear. But it wasn't clear what she had in mind.

Now it was.

Chapter Twelve

"Clarice," he said, running his eyes over the curves and shadows of her bountiful, lovely body. He hadn't heard her sing yet, but her beauty had to be one of the reasons for her success. "Are you sure about this?"

"I want to turn my brain off," she said, coming closer to him. "Don't you?"

He put his hands on her shoulders, then ran them around to her back and down to her bare butt.

"Well, now that you mention it . . ."

He wrapped his arms around her, pulled her close and kissed her. She went to encircle him with her arms around his waist, but encountered his gun. He had worn the holster in case he ran into the glaring man, or killer.

"Sorry," he said. He backed up, unstrapped the belt and laid it down within reach.

Instead of coming back into his arms she busied herself removing his shirt. She ran her mouth and hands over his chest, then went to work removing the remainder of his clothes.

When he was totally nude, she backed up and looked at him. His cock was hard and full and she studied it with shiny, hungry eyes.

Eagerly, she sank to her knees in front of him and rubbed her cheeks with his cock, reveling in the heat of it. Then she encircled it with one hand and stroked it while cupping his heavy sack in her other hand. Finally, she opened her mouth and stuck her tongue out to wet the spongy tip. When she had it gleaming with her saliva, she took the column into her mouth and worked to accommodate the entire length.

Clint closed his eyes and did what Clarice said—or tried to. He couldn't turn off his mind completely, not while there was possible danger outside the door. But he did try to give himself up to the sensations of her mouth, tongue and fingers. When he thought he wouldn't be able to hold back any further he reached down to slip his hands underneath her arms and lift her to her feet. But he didn't leave her there long, picking her up in his arms.

"That way," she said, pointing, and pressing her mouth to his neck.

He carried her to the doorway she indicated and into the bedroom. The bed seemed vast and would give them plenty of room to roll around on. He set her down on her back, then slid onto the bed with her. He took the time to explore her body with his hands and mouth, and as he groaned appreciatively, worked his way down between her smooth, creamy thighs.

He kissed her, breathed in her scent, and then buried his face in her wet pussy. He worked avidly with his tongue and lips, and before long he drove her over the edge so that she nearly screamed, her heels drumming on the mattress.

Getting to his knees, he mounted her and drove himself deep into her wet depths, which was growing wetter still, soaking the sheets beneath them. As he drove in and out of her, she wrapped her legs around his waist and found his rhythm so she could match it. From there they each emptied their minds and sought their own release . . .

***

"My God," she said later, still breathless, "that was just what I wanted."

"Happy to oblige," he said, lying with one hand behind his head. He turned his face to look at her. She was mussed and beautiful.

"Can you stay?" she asked.

"How long?"

"All night?"

"Why?"

She put one hand out and stroked his flaccid cock.

"So we can do this again, silly."

"I can certainly stay for that," he said. "In the morning I'll have to go to my room for my belongings, and then we'll head for the train."

She moved over to press her body against him, and put her head on his shoulder. She left her hand on his crotch.

"Oh, my," she said.

"What?"

"You're almost ready to go again."

He looked down at himself and said, "So I am."

She giggled. It was the only time since meeting her that he heard her laugh.

***

Some time during the night he went out to the main room to get his gun and bring it into the bedroom.

"You're going to need more than that to keep me away from you," she said, as he hung it on the bedpost.

"Maybe I think I'll need it to keep you off of me," he said.

"Do you think you'll want to keep me off of you?" she asked.

He got back in bed next to her and said, "Hell no."

Chapter Thirteen

The night was an exhausting one. Clarice's appetite for sex seemed nonending, but they both assumed they'd rest on the train.

When Clint and Clarice got to the lobby with bell-boys carrying their luggage, Clint was amazed at how many bags and trunks the songstress had.

"I may not have my own musicians," she said, when she saw his face, "but everything else is mine."

Inspector Meade arrived and had his men help the bellman take the luggage out to a carriage. When it was all loaded, she settled her bill and thanked the Waldorf staff for their service. Outside Meade rode in a carriage with them, with the luggage in a second carriage with his men.

Meade had his men load the luggage onto the train, then stood there alertly while Clint and Clarice boarded.

"I hope the trip goes well," he told them.

"Thank you, Inspector," Clarice said. "You've been very kind."

Clint walked Clarice to her sleeping car.

"You can stay here with me, you know," she told him. "We don't have any secrets from each other, and the bunk looks cozy."

"The bunk looks tight," he said. "Don't worry, I'll be in here with you most of the time. I'm going to want to have a good look at people in the dining car."

As they sat across from each other she asked, "How long is this part of the trip?"

"Pittsburgh's about four hundred miles," he said. "It'll depend on how often they need to stop for water. If they have it stored in a teller car, it might be three nights. If they don't carry water, they might have to make a stop every seven to ten miles."

"Oh, my," she said. "Three nights doesn't sound too bad, but . . ."

"We'll keep our fingers crossed," he said.

They sat and watched as the cityscape went by and quickly turned to open country. They each had a bag with some small, personal items in them, although Clarice's was three times the size of Clint's, which was really just a saddlebag.

He switched seats to sit next to her and they dozed that way a bit, with her head on his shoulder. The night's romantic exertions was still weighing on both of them.

When Clint woke, it was getting dark, so he decided to check the dining car, see who was there, and bring some food back to Clarice. He told her to keep the door locked.

***

Clint walked through one of the passenger cars to the dining car. He didn't see anyone suspicious, although it was crowded with people of all kinds. There were men and women traveling alone, couples together, families with children. They studied him as he walked by, but it was just out of boredom.

"Would you like a table, sir?" a white jacket wearing black waiter asked him.

"No, I'd like to take some food back to my compartment, if I may."

"You can go up to the bar in the front of the car and order."

"Thank you," Clint said.

He walked through the car, exchanging gazes with the diners. A lovely woman sitting alone, eating a slice of pie, gave him a come hither smile. He smiled back but kept walking. However, he was thinking about the pie she was eating. He wondered if it was peach. He stopped and walked back.

"Excuse me," he said to her.

The woman looked up at him and smiled, her eyes bright.

"Hello."

"I'm sorry to bother you, but is that peach? Pie?"

"Why yes, it is." Her hair was pitch black and her eyes sky blue. If Clarice hadn't been waiting for him, he would have sat down across from her.

"It's my favorite. How is it?" he asked.

"It's very good. Would you like to sit and join me?"

He almost did but resisted.

"Sorry, I can't."

"Oh well," she said, with a shrug, "maybe later."

"Maybe. Enjoy your pie."

"You, too . . . sir?"

"Clint."

She nodded and he continued to walk. When he reached the bar, a couple of men holding drinks stepped aside.

"A drink, sir?" the black bartender asked.

"A beer, while I wait for some food."

"Of course." The bartender handed him the beer. "What would you like?"

"Two steak dinners, and I'll take them back to my compartment."

"Right away, sir."

Clint sipped his beer and said, "Oh yeah, two pieces of peach pie, too."

Chapter Fourteen

With the help of a porter, Clint returned to the compartment with two steak dinners, two pieces of peach pie, and coffee.

"No wine?" she complained, but he saw that she was kidding.

It was difficult to cut their steaks while balancing plates on their laps, so eventually they sat across from each other and set their plates down on the seats next to them.

"This is certainly not worth the effort," Clarice said, struggling to chew.

Clint agreed completely, but was surprised when it came to the peach pie, which was delicious. Clarice tried to doctor her coffee with cream and a lot of sugar, but for Clint hot and black was fine.

"You don't seem like a dessert person to me," she observed.

"I'm not," he said, "I prefer a good steak, but in the absence of that, it's nice to find some good peach pie."

"I prefer apple," Clarice said.

"Next time," he assured her.

With the help of the same young porter, they cleared the remnants of the meal from the compartment and once again sat side-by-side.

"Did you meet anyone interesting in the other cars?" she asked.

"None in the passenger car I passed through," Clint said, "but I met a lady."

"Pretty?"

"Very."

"What did she want?" Clarice asked.

"She invited me to join her over a slice of peach pie."

"And did you?"

"No," he said. "Not with you waiting here."

"Then I feel sorry for her," she said. "Maybe I should go to the dining car and spend some time with her."

"She's probably not there anymore."

"Does she have a compartment?"

"We didn't get that far."

"What about her name?"

"We only exchanged first names," Clint said. "Hers was Rebecca."

"Pretty name."

"It's just as well," Clint said. "We want to keep you out of sight."

"I guess so." She went to her bag. "If you don't mind, I'm going to get ready for bed."

"I'll take a walk."

"You don't have to."

"No, you deserve some privacy," he said. "I'll check out the other end of train."

"Do you know what's back there?"

"Probably a stock car," Clint said, "and their water, if they're carrying any."

"Then I'll see you in a little while," she said. "Be careful."

***

Clint walked to the back of the train, through the baggage car, stock car, and teller car to the caboose, where he stepped outside. He breathed in the fresh air, wondering if the killer of Leo Delaware had watched him walk by? Would he now watch him walk back? Or might he still be in a forward car?

He went back into the caboose and started his walk back. Along the way, in the hall of a passenger car, he encountered another porter.

"Can I help you find somethin', suh?" the black man asked.

"No," Clint said, "I'm just stretching my legs."

"Yes, suh." The porter started walking away.

"Just a minute," he called.

The man stopped and turned.

"Yes, suh?"

"Where would I find the conductor?"

"This away, suh."

He followed the porter forward. Before they got to the dining car, the porter stopped and knocked on a door. It was opened by a thick-set white man in his fifties."

"Can I help you, sir?" the man asked.

"Yes," Clint said. "I just had a few questions."

The conductor looked past Clint at the porter.

"You can go, Gus," the man said.

"Yasshuh." The porter said and left.

"Come inside, sir," the conductor said backing up. It was a small, cramped room, made moreso by the fact that there were now two inside. The conductor moved to a table, sat at it and looked up at Clint.

"What can I do for you, sir?"

"I was just wondering who the law on this train is?" Clint asked.

"That would be me. Is there a problem?"

"No, not really," Clint said. "I just wanted to know who would be in charge if there was."

"I would be, until we pulled into a stop that had some real law," the man said. "My name is Biggs."

"Just Biggs?"

"Mister Biggs. If you need anythin', just let me know."

"I will."

"Is there anythin' else? I have work to do."

"No," Clint said. "I don't want to keep you from your work. Thanks."

Clint left the room, leaving Biggs to the papers on his desk.

Chapter Fifteen

Clint knocked and Clarice opened the door for him. She had changed into one of her silk robes.

"Did you find anything? Anyone?"

"I found a conductor," Clint said. "Walked my way to the rear of the train."

"Did you find your lady friend?"

"No," Clint said, "and she's not my lady friend."

Clarice sat on the bunk, which had folded down from above.

"You were right," she said.

"About what?"

"The bed is cramped."

"That's okay," Clint said. "I can sleep in the passenger car. There are seats available."

"I guess we can make it work,"

"I want you to sleep comfortably and well," he said. "You'll need your rest if you're going to perform."

"But what about if we don't want to sleep?" she asked.

"We have plenty of hotel rooms available, and a woman of your stature will get the best ones available. With large beds."

She slid into the bunk beneath the sheets and said, "If you change your mind, come on back."

"Good night."

Clint left the compartment and waited while she got out of bed and locked the door, then walked down the hall, smiling.

He decided to go back to the dining car, which at this time of night was mostly empty. However, Rebecca was sitting at the same table, either still or again. She smiled as he came down the aisle.

"Bringing food back to the compartment, again, Clint?" she asked him.

"Not this time," he said.

"Then perhaps you'd care to join me?"

"Of course."

He sat across from her, and a waiter hurried over.

"Peach pie, please, with tea," she said.

"I'll have a slice of peach pie also," Clint said, "but with black coffee."

"Yes, suh."

"You look more relaxed," she said.

"Did I look tense before?"

"A bit," she said. "You studied everyone in the car. Were you lookin' for someone in particular, or just trouble?"

"I'm always looking for trouble," he said. "Or rather, I'm on the lookout for it."

"It must be hard, being known as The Gunsmith." She saw his surprise.

"I didn't know my presence was generally known."

"Them waiters have their own grapevine," she said.

"How do you know that?"

"I travel by train very often," she said.

"For business or pleasure?"

"Both."

The waiter came with their pie and drinks.

"Thank you," she said, then looked at Clint. "I've traveled for both."

"What business are you in?"

"I'm a journalist."

"Oh? What newspaper do you work for?"

"I work for a service that owns many newspapers," she said. "My column appears in all of them."

"That's very impressive," Clint said. "I'll have to look for it. What's your next column going to be about?"

"Someone you know, I think," Rebecca said. "A lady named Clarice DuPont."

Clint sat back in his chair.

"You know about her?"

"I know she's on this train, and she's starting a tour in Pittsburgh. I'm going to be at her first show."

"And then what?"

"And then I go where she goes," Rebecca said. "And, I assume, where you go."

"So you knew who I was when we met?"

She nodded.

"I saw you get on the train," she said.

"You knew what I looked like?"

She nodded again.

"I'd seen you once before," she said, "and you're not easy to forget."

"So what is it you want?" he asked. "Certainly more than just sharing a slice of peach pie?"

"A front row seat," she said, "or a special box."

"And what do I get in return?"

"An honest review."

"A good review?"

Rebecca laughed.

"I said honest," she said. "I'd have to see, first. So whatya say?"

"If that's all you're asking," Clint said, "I don't see why not?"

Rebecca picked up her tea and held it aloft in a salute.

Chapter Sixteen

Other people drifted in and out of the dining car, probably unable to sleep. A cup of coffee, or a drink, and then they went off to try again. But Clint and Rebecca stayed and got acquainted.

Her last name was Moreau, and she had been a journalist for ten years. Working her way up to the point where she now had her own column all over the country, telling people what they should see and what they should not see.

Clint told very little of his story, but enough to contradict a lot of what Rebecca had read about him.

"So you *are* friends with legendary gunmen," she commented, "but you're not one yourself."

"That's right."

She laughed.

"What's funny?" he asked.

"I think you're either kidding yourself, or you're very modest."

"I'm not modest."

"Well then, maybe you just don't know your own reputation, very well."

"I know my reputation just fine," he assured her. "I just know my real nature."

"Speaking of your real nature," Rebecca said, "escorting a theater actress and singer on her tour doesn't strike me as the Gunsmith's sort of task."

"There's more to it," he said.

"Really?" she asked. "Like what?"

"If I told you that," he said, "it'd end up in all your columns."

Rebecca hesitated, then admitted, "Yes, it would."

"Then let's just say she needed an escort who knew something about the West."

"Well," she said, "that certainly fits your description."

"Yes, it does."

"Let me ask you another question."

"Go ahead."

"Why are you here while she's in a sleeping compartment? I presume alone?"

"She needs her rest."

"So," Rebecca went on, slowly, "she's not expecting you back any time soon?"

"Not til early morning, when I bring the lady her breakfast."

"That's interesting. It sounds like she's got you well trained."

"Just part of the service."

"What else is part of the service?" Rebecca asked with a sly smile.

"I guess I'll find that out as we go along."

They finished their pie and stood up to leave the dining car.

"Do you have a compartment?" he asked her. "I'll walk you there."

"No," she said, touching his arm, "but I kind of wish I did. I'm just sitting in the passenger car."

"So am I," he said. "So I'll walk you there. Maybe we can find two seats together."

"Close together would be nice," she said, and they left the car.

***

As it turned out, they did find two seats together, with no one seated across from them.

"Let's ask the conductor for a blanket," she whispered as they sat.

"It's not cold," he commented.

"No," she said, "it's not."

As Mr. Biggs walked by, Clint asked for a blanket.

***

As they spread the blanket out across their laps Rebecca snuggled up closer to him. Without preamble, she put one hand on his thigh and started to rub. Before long she was massaging his burgeoning cock through his trousers. Clint could only hope that Clarice didn't come walking into the car at that point.

"Do you mind?" she asked.

"I don't mind at all."

"No," she said, taking his hand and putting it on her leg, "neither would I." She was wearing a skirt of moderate length, so that his hand was actually on her bare leg.

With amazing alacrity, she managed to unbutton his trousers, avoid his gunbelt, and slide her hand inside to grasp his cock. To return the favor he moved his hand up her inner thigh so he could slide inside her underwear, where he found her wet and waiting. As she continued to work his cock to fullness, he slid his middle finger inside her wet pussy and moved it around. They both saw that no one was paying them any mind, they increased their ministrations of each other until they had very wet and sticky hands . . .

Chapter Seventeen

In turn they each went to the train's facility to clean up. Eventually, they dozed, Rebecca with her head on Clint's shoulder. In the morning they moved apart and stretched.

"That was a pleasant night," Rebecca said.

"Not something I ever expected."

Rebecca smiled.

"I bet your lady is waiting for her breakfast."

"You're right," Clint said. "I have to go." He stood and slid by her.

"Will I see you later?" she asked. "In the dining car?"

"I'm sure."

He went to the dining car to fetch breakfast for himself and Clarice.

***

He carried the plates himself, knocked on the compartment door with his foot.

"Good morning," she said, opening the door. "I was wondering."

"There'll be a porter along with some coffee," Clint said. "I thought you'd be hungry."

"You're right."

He entered and they sat across from each other with their plates. Clarice had already folded the bunk up.

"How did you sleep sitting up?" she asked.

"Pretty well, actually?"

"Did you see your lady friend?"

"You'll find this ironic," he said, and told her who Rebecca was.

"Well," she replied, "I hope you were nice to her if we need a good review."

"I did my best," he told her, which he found ironic.

The porter arrived with a pot of coffee and two cups. Clint thanked him and tipped him. They finished eating, watching the prairie and occasional structures go by.

When they finished eating, they put the plates on one seat and shared the other one.

"I have an idea," she said.

"What's that?"

"I'd like to meet this Rebecca Moreau."

"You want to leave this compartment?" he asked.

"Well," Clarice said, "you haven't seen anyone suspicious."

"I have a better idea," Clint said. "I'll bring her to you."

"I'll have to clean this place up," Clarice said, "as well as myself, but that should work."

Clint looked around. The compartment seemed clean enough to him, and he knew Clarice would dress well.

"She's probably in the dining car having her own breakfast," Clint said. "How long will you need?"

"Give me an hour."

Clint thought that was pretty long, but he knew his idea of clean was not hers.

"Okay," he said. "I'll get rid of all these breakfast things."

"Maybe you could have a porter bring a pot of tea and some cups," Clarice said.

"I'll take care of it."

He collected the plates and cups and left.

***

He found Rebecca at the same table in the dining car. He started to bring the plates and cups to the front of the car, but a porter met him and relieved him of them. That done, he sat across from Rebecca, who looked to be having a hearty breakfast of bacon-and-eggs.

"How's Miss DuPont?" she asked.

"She's fine," Clint said." She's had breakfast and thought it might be a good idea for you two to meet."

"Really?"

"Yes," Clint said. "She's invited you to her compartment for tea."

"When?"

"In about an hour."

"That works," Rebecca said. "I'd be delighted."

"I'll let her know."

"Could you also ask her if we could do a casual interview?" Rebecca asked.

Clint stood and said, "I'll ask her. I should be right back."

"I'm gonna keep eating til then," she said. "Something happened last night that seems to have given me an appetite."

"Must've been something strenuous," he said, and left . . .

***

Clarice approved Rebecca's requests for an interview. She thought it was a good idea.

"Especially if her column is in so many newspapers."

Clint returned to the dining car to collect Rebecca.

Chapter Eighteen

Rebecca had finished her breakfast by the time Clint returned, and they sat there for a good half hour more to give Clarice time to get ready.

"Let's not keep your lady waiting any longer," Rebecca then said, and they rose and left the car.

When they reached the compartment, Clint knocked and Clarice slid the door open. She had dressed in a very professional looking suit and done her hair up. She looked lovely and professional. Rebecca was wearing a very businesslike suit.

"Clarice DuPont," Clint said, "meet Miss Rebecca Moreau."

"Miss DuPont," Rebecca said, "how do you do?"

"It's a pleasure to meet you, Miss Moreau," Clarice responded. "Please, come in."

Rebecca entered, and as Clint moved to follow, Clarice stopped him.

"Clint," she said, "I think Miss Moreau and I would like to be alone."

"Oh, of course," Clint said. "I understand."

"Perhaps you could go back to the dining car for some coffee and we'll let you know when we've finished."

"Fine," Clint said, and she slid the door closed.

Clint walked to the dining car, assuming Rebecca would have done the same thing to Clarice's manager, if he had been there.

***

In the dining car, Clint sat and ordered a cup of coffee. He hoped the two women were getting along and being very professional with each other. He didn't want them comparing notes about anything else.

Clint watched as men and women went by, in and out of the car. He still didn't see anyone resembling Clarice's description of the glaring man, and didn't spot anyone who looked the least bit suspicious.

He didn't have any idea how long to give the two ladies, so he determined to simply sit where he was until one of them appeared. In time that's just what happened. Rebecca walked into the car and joined him at his table.

"All finished?" he asked.

"Oh, yes," Rebecca said. "She's a lovely girl. We had a nice little conversation."

"Really?" Clint asked. "What did you talk about?"

"Are you worried that we talked about you?" Rebecca asked, looking amused.

"No, of course not."

"Don't worry," she said. "I didn't tell her what happened beneath our blanket. We just had a pleasant discussion about her career, and her plans for the future."

Clint wondered if Clarice had told Rebecca about Leo Delaware's murder, but Rebecca never mentioned it.

"She told me to tell you that you could go back, now," Rebecca said.

"We have to talk about what will happen when we reach Pittsburgh," he said, standing.

Rebecca took out a small notebook and said, "I'm just going to sit here and arrange my thoughts for my column. I hope I'll see you later."

"I'm sure you will," he said, and headed back to Clarice's compartment.

***

When Clarice opened the door for him, she did so wordlessly, then turned away. He entered and slid the door shut behind him.

"How did it go?" he asked, as she seated herself by the window.

"Very well," she said. "She's a very professional woman."

"How much did you cover with her?" he asked. "She was here a while."

"We talked about my career, and where I was going," Clarice said. "Some of it I wasn't really very sure of, since Leo was killed."

"Did you mention him?"

"No," Clarice said, "I didn't want to touch on that."

Clint sat across from her.

"Anything else?"

Clarice glared at him.

"You mean the fact that you slept with her last night?" she demanded.

"Did she tell you that?"

"She didn't have to tell me," Clarice said. "I could see it and feel it."

"Now, Clarice," he said. "We sat next to each other last night in a passenger car, and we both slept. That doesn't mean we slept together."

"You mean you didn't have sex with her last night?"

Clint didn't answer the question directly.

"Where would we have done that?" Clint asked. "Neither of us has a compartment, and we sat in a crowded passenger car." It wasn't so crowded, but that wasn't the point. "Why'd you get that into your head?"

“She’s a beautiful woman,” Clarice said. “And she had . . . an attitude.”

Clarice folded her arms beneath her breasts and frowned.

“If this is going to bother you so much, Clarice, maybe we better make our relationship strictly business.”

“No,” she cried, unfolding her arms, “no, it’ll be all right. I won’t play the jealous female, I promise.”

“That’s good,” Clint said. “Now maybe we should just talk about what we’re going to do when we reach Pittsburgh, which should be sometime tomorrow afternoon.”

Chapter Nineteen

Clint tried to maintain a sexless relationship with both women the rest of the way. It wasn't hard with Rebecca, since the passenger cars were full the rest of the way, as they stopped to pick up more passengers. It wasn't possible to do anything, even beneath a blanket. And he continued to talk about the cramped quarters of Clarice's compartment.

He knew he probably should have maintained this kind of relationship with Clarice all along, but he felt she had needed a shoulder to lean on in the aftermath of her manager's death. Maybe, in Pittsburgh, where she had to be in shape—body and mind—to perform, their relationship could change.

He decided to try something and see how she reacted. He told her he would bring supper to her compartment that night, but he would have his own in the dining car.

"With Rebecca?" she demanded.

"I intend to eat alone," he told her.

"I'm sorry," she said, "I'm sorry . . . I won't be like that again."

He wasn't so sure. As long as Rebecca was around, he didn't know if Clarice could avoid feeling jealous. He had already made a couple of mistakes in his handling of this trip. He hoped he wouldn't make anymore.

***

Luckily, with the addition of more passengers, the dining car was crowded. Clint made sure when he sat down to eat, there was no room at his table when Rebecca appeared. She ended up sharing a table with another woman traveling with her two small children.

Likewise, since he got to the passenger car first, he managed to sit with people all around him. Rebecca ended sitting with the same woman she had shared a table with in the dining car.

The next morning Clint brought breakfast for both he and Clarice to the compartment. Clarice did not mention Rebecca through the meal, and Clint did not know just how hard an effort that took.

Clarice had her bags all packed and ready by the time they pulled into Pittsburgh, and managed to avoid seeing Rebecca as they disembarked.

They got a carriage in front of the train station and Clint gave the driver the name of the hotel on Leo Delaware's written itinerary.

Clarice was looking around as they pulled away, and Clint was convinced she was looking for Rebecca.

***

They pulled up in front of the Marigold Hotel, which took up a large part of a fairly busy street. Several bell-boys came running out to help them with their luggage. Another man, this one well-dressed and wearing a bow-tie, rushed to introduce himself as the assistant manager and welcome them to the hotel.

"Welcome, welcome," he cried out. "My name is Victor, and I'm the Assistant Manager. We are so proud to have you in our establishment, Miss DuPont." He looked at Clint. "You and your manager, Mr. Delaware."

"Thank you," Clarice said, "but this is not Mr. Delaware. He . . . didn't make the trip. This is Mr. Adams."

"Welcome, Mr. Adams," Victor said. "We have both your rooms ready."

"Miss DuPont should have a suite," Clint reminded him.

"Of course," Victor said, "A suite for the lady, and a room for you."

"That's fine."

"This way, then," Victor said, "the boys are already on their way up with your bags."

Clint and Clarice followed the young assistant manager up the front steps and into the hotel.

The lobby was large, with a high ceiling and heavily decorated with plants. Victor led them to a stairway, up to the second floor and down a hall.

"Miss DuPont's suite is here, your room is down the hall," Victor said, "but only a few doors away."

"Fine," Clint said.

Victor took them into the suite as the bellboys were leaving, having delivered the bags. Clint tipped them all generously.

"I hope this is to your liking," the assistant manager said.

"It's lovely," Clarice said, looking around. She walked to the doorway of the bedroom and glanced inside.

"This bed is one of our new ones, brought in from Baltimore. It's very comfortable and large."

"I can see," she said. "And Mr. Adams' bed?"

"Also comfortable and large, but not as new."

"That's fine," Clint said.

"Take him to his room," Clarice said. "I want to get settled." She looked at Clint. "See you in a while."

"This way, sir," Victor said.

Chapter Twenty

Victor walked Clint down the hall two doors and used a key to unlock the door. It was much smaller than Clarice's suite, but larger than most hotel rooms.

"I hope this is satisfactory."

"It's fine," Clint said. His saddlebags were on the bed, which meant he had everything he needed.

"I can have the chef prepare lunch for you and Miss DuPont."

"That would be good, Victor," Clint said, "but please have it served in her suite."

"As you wish. There are also some musicians from the theater waiting to see the two of you."

"Yes, they'll want to see her," Clint said. "I suggest you include them when you serve lunch."

"Excellent idea," the man said. "I will let you know when we are ready to serve."

"Thank you."

Victor executed a half bow and left. Clint took the time to wash up and change his shirt, then walked down the hall to Clarice's suite. He knocked on her door and it opened immediately.

"Happy with your accommodations?" Clint asked.

"They're fine." She had freshened up and put on a robe.

"We're going to be having lunch here with some musicians."

"That's good. I do need to talk with them and rehearse. I'll also need to speak with their band leader."

"That's stuff Leo would've handled, right?"

"Yes," she said. "I don't expect you to do it. I can handle it."

"And when do we go and look at the theater?" he asked.

"I'll arrange that with them."

"And when's the performance?"

"Day after tomorrow."

"And we'll have to go through this at every stop?" he asked.

"We will." She looked at him with a very serious expression, her arms folded. "Clint, we won't be able to have sex anymore. I can't be . . . distracted."

"I understand."

"So, if you want to see Rebecca—"

"Clarice, there's nothing going on with Rebecca. You just concentrate on what you have to do, and I'll concentrate on keeping you safe."

"That sounds right."

"Lunch should be in about an hour. I'll leave you to get ready."

"And so," she said, "it all begins."

Clint went back to his own room.

***

When Victor came to Clint's room to tell him lunch was ready to be delivered to Clarice's room, he instructed the man to bring the musicians to him, first. When they arrived there were five of them, none of whom resembled Clarice's description of the glaring man. They did not have any instruments with them, but Clint assumed they and Clarice would interact just the same.

He figured he would just watch. He took them down the hall and introduced them.

Victor arrived with bellboys carrying a table and many plates of food. They set them up, and before long Clarice and the musicians were seated, eating and discussing what would happen at the theater. Clint ate and listened to them with half an ear. A lot of it didn't make sense to him.

One man told Clarice that their bandleader, a man named Starke, was looking forward to meeting with her in the theater. Clarice told him that would happen the next morning.

All through the meal she and the musicians went through a list of songs. From what Clint could understand, they managed to find songs they all knew.

After the musicians left, Clint sat with Clarice over coffee.

“We don’t go to the theater until tomorrow?” Clint asked. “Why not tonight?”

“The bandleader isn’t available until tomorrow. But I’ll use tonight to go through my playlist.”

“Then you’ll need to be alone.”

“Yes. But this was lunch. Let’s have dinner just the two of us, here tonight. We still have things to discuss.”

“All right,” he said.

“Eight o’clock?”

“That’s fine,” Clint said. “But to eat and make plans, right?”

“Yes, that’s all,” she said.

“Then I’ll see you later,” he said. “I’ll wheel this table out into the hall for the bellboys to pick up.”

She held the door open for him while he pushed the table out, then said, “See you later.”

She closed the door.

Chapter Twenty-One

Clint returned to his own room, but remained there for only a few minutes. He decided to go out into the streets of Pittsburgh and have a look around. In the lobby he encountered Victor.

"Can I help you, sir?" the assistant manager asked. "The boys have gone up to clean the suite."

"That's fine," Clint said. "I thought I'd take a walk. Can you tell me where the theater is?"

"It's a pretty long walk, sir," Victor said. "I would suggest a carriage. I can have one brought around for you, with or without a driver."

"With, I think," Clint said. "Thank you."

"Right away, sir."

Within five minutes a carriage, being pulled by a single horse, stopped in front of the hotel. A doorman appeared to hold the door open so Clint could enter.

"The theater, sir?" the doorman asked Clint.

"Yes."

The doorman told the driver, "The theater!"

The carriage pulled away and carried Clint through the busy streets of Pittsburgh, until it stopped in front of the Majestic Theater. Clint had not intended to visit the theater, so there was no word called ahead. As he entered, he realized he didn't even know the bandleader's name. However, as luck would have it, he saw a couple of the musicians he had met at lunch, and then they came to the edge of the stage to greet him as he approached.

"Mr. Adams," one said. "What brings you here?"

"Since I'm in charge of security for Miss DuPont, I wanted to take a look at the theater beforehand."

"Hey, no problem," the other musician said. "We can show you around."

"Thanks, I'd appreciate it."

"Why don't we start backstage?"

***

The two musicians showed Clint the backstage area, the dressing rooms, various doors in and out of the theater, access to the rafters and roof of the building. They showed him the box office area, different doors that gave access to the seats, where the band gathered and played, then returned with him to the front of the stage.

"Is the bandleader here?" Clint asked. "I didn't see him or his dressing room."

"That would be Mr. Starke. He's here somewhere. I saw him this mornin'. I know he'll want to speak with you."

"I'd be obliged."

The man went off to look. The second man remained with Clint.

"What kind of fella is this Starke?" Clint asked him.

"He's kinda strict, wants things done just his way. He don't take no guff from nobody."

"Do you fellas like him?" Clint asked.

"We respect him, but some of us are afraid of him."

"Is he from this area?"

"No, that's part of his attitude, I guess," the man said "He's from the East, where they do things different. They even dress different."

"Dress how?"

"Well, for instance, he wears a black cape. The further west he gets, he's gonna stand out."

"Is he moving west?"

"He made it pretty clear when he came here a few months ago that this was a temporary stop for him. The rest of us are here for life . . . Ah, here he comes."

The other musician was coming down the aisle from the rear of the theater, followed by a short, big-bellied man wearing a red-lined black cape.

"Mr. Adams," the musician said, "this is our band leader, Mr. Starke."

"Mr. Adams," Stark said in a high, almost whiny voice, "happy to meet you."

The man's hand was very moist and soft, but the handshake itself surprisingly firm.

"I assume Miss DuPont is not here?"

"No, she's not," Clint said. "In fact, I hadn't even planned to come this afternoon, but I was out so I thought I'd have a look. These two gents were nice enough to show me around."

"For security purposes, I understand."

"Yes, that's my responsibility."

"I understand perfectly. Well, I assume the only thing you haven't seen is my dressing room. I'll be happy to show it to you, as it has a door to the outside."

"That'd be great."

He looked at the musicians and said, "You two can go back to rehearsal."

"Yes, sir."

As they walked away, Clint said, "I didn't hear any rehearsing."

"They couldn't do it as long as they were showing you around," Starke said. "They should get to it now. This way, please."

Chapter Twenty-Two

After Starke had shown Clint around his dressing room—including the door that led to the alley—he took a bottle of whiskey from the bottom drawer of his dressing table and poured two glasses. Although Clint was not fond of whiskey, he drank with the man.

"If you don't mind me saying so, sir," Starke said, "you don't look like a man whose preference runs to the theater."

"You're absolutely right," Clint said. "This is new territory for me."

"I thought I recognized your name," Starke said. "You are the Gunsmith, correct?"

"Yes, sir," Clint said.

"What are you doing in the theater?"

"Miss DuPont was concerned about her safety as she travels west. I agreed to provide her security."

"She is very lucky," Starke said. "I imagine you will keep the lady very safe."

"That's my intention." He put his empty glass down.

"Another?"

"I don't think so," Clint said. "I should get back to the hotel. Thank you and your men for the hospitality."

"We are looking forward to working with the lady," Starke said. "We'll see her tomorrow?"

"Definitely."

The two men shook hands and then Clint made his way out of the theater and to the carriage.

***

The carriage left him off in front of the hotel, where he was greeted by the doorman. In the ornate lobby he stopped at the front desk.

"Has Miss DuPont been looking for me?" he asked the desk clerk.

"No, sir, we haven't heard a word from the lady, at all."

"Thank you." That was good. He hadn't intended to go out or be gone that long. It was just as well she didn't know he had left.

He went back to his room. There was still some time before dinner, so he decided to wash up, then spend some time with Mark Twain.

***

He thought he heard some commotion in the hall. He checked and saw a bellboy wheeling a table into

Clarice's suite. He went back into his room to strap on his gun, then left and walked down the hall. Clarice, dressed elegantly with her hair hanging down, opened the door and smiled.

"Good evening," she greeted him.

"Good evening."

He stepped in and she closed the door and gestured.

"The table is set. Shall we?"

"Definitely," he said. "I'm starved."

He held her chair, then sat across from her.

"What did you do today, Clint?"

"I meant to go for a walk," Clint said, "but I ended up going to the theater."

"Why did you do that without me?" she asked, pausing over her roast chicken.

"Security purposes," Clint said. "I had a look at all the entrances and exits there were. I also got to know a couple of the musicians a bit better."

"If you showed up there unannounced, it means you interrupted their rehearsal."

"That's true."

"The band leader couldn't have been very pleased about that."

"That would be Starke," Clint said. "I met him, as well."

"Did you?" she asked. Clint couldn't tell if she was angry or not. "What's he like?"

"A little round man in a red-lined cape," Clint said. "I didn't see him in action, but his musicians seem to either respect or fear him."

"That sounds like most of the bandleaders I've worked with," she said.

"Well, he's looking forward to meeting you."

"That'll be tomorrow morning," she said. "That's when we'll go over my list of songs."

"And will he have time to go over them with his band?"

"He better," she said.

***

After dinner they agreed on a time to meet in her suite tomorrow morning for breakfast. Afterward Clint would get them a carriage to the theater for Clarice to meet with the band leader, Starke.

"Is that what we have to do at every stop?" he asked her.

"I'm afraid so," she said. "These are all new locations for me."

"Alright," he said, "at least I'll get the pattern down pat."

There was no conversation about their sleeping together. Apparently, they had both moved on in their relationship.

Chapter Twenty-Three

Clint woke the next morning after a refreshing night's sleep. Keeping a professional relationship with Clarice was certainly less stressful.

After a pleasant breakfast, he walked her down to the front of the hotel and the doorman got them a carriage. They got in the back and told the driver to take them to the Majestic Theater.

"During the ride Clarice said, "When we arrive I'll talk with Mr. Starke alone. You're not involved in this part."

"That suits me," Clint said.

When the carriage stopped in front of the theater, they disembarked under the watchful eyes of some people on the street who pointed, oohed and awed.

"Apparently, your reputation precedes you," Clint said.

"That makes me think," she said. "When we get further west, will your reputation precede you?"

"We'll have to wait and see."

When they entered the theater, Clint heard music coming from the stage. Standing in front was the portly figure of Mr. Starke. The man heard them coming down the aisle and turned.

"Ah, good-morning, Mr. Adams," he greeted.

"Good morning, Mr. Starke. I'd like you to meet Miss Clarice DuPont."

"Miss DuPont," Starke said, taking her hand. "A pleasure."

"Mr. Starke," she said, as they shook hands.

"I'll leave you to it and take a walk around outside," Clint said.

"Why don't we go backstage to my dressing room where we can be alone and discuss your playlist," Starke said.

"Very well," she said, and off they walked.

Clint turned and went back up the aisle and through the door.

***

Outside he found people strolling past, not paying him much attention as he came out.

There weren't any other buildings very close to the theater, which stood virtually alone. Anyone wanting to cause trouble would have to get inside, for they would be conspicuous outside.

Clint saw no reason to leave the theater area, so he simply walked around the entire building one time, checking doors and windows as he passed them and finding them locked.

Before long, he was back in front of the theater. There seemed to be no one interested in him or the building, and certainly no man resembling the glaring man.

Clint decided to wait in front of the theater and folded his arms, keeping his eyes wide open until Clarice appeared again.

***

Inside, Starke gave Clarice a glass of wine while they sat and talked, planning their program. When they were done, he put the music sheets aside, and poured them each another glass of wine.

"I'm intrigued by your choice of the Gunsmith as a traveling companion."

"Because he's not musical?"

"Indeed."

"My manager thought it might be necessary to come West with someone who knew his way around the West," she said. "Then he was killed, and I thought it wise to have someone who could not only show me around the territory, but protect me, as well."

"I see," Starke said. "Are you telling me that my musicians and myself might be in danger?"

"Not at all," she said. "It's just that in New York someone seemed to take an interest in me."

"And that person killed your manager?"

"We don't know for sure," she said. "The police there are looking into it. Meanwhile, I travel with Clint."

"Then I suppose you've done the right thing," he said. "First performance seven tomorrow night?"

"Yes."

"I'll walk you back out to Mr. Adams."

He took her glass, set it and his own aside, and led her from his dressing room.

***

When Starke and Clarice came out of the theater, Clint straightened and faced them.

"All set?"

"We are prepared for the lady's debut on our stage," Starke said. He bowed to Clarice. "I have sent one of my men for a carriage. Until tomorrow."

She nodded and he went into the theater.

"Did you sing for him?" Clint asked.

"I didn't have to."

"How does he know if you're good enough for his theater?"

"It doesn't matter," she said. "I'm booked, and there will be ticket sales. If he doesn't like me, he'll just never have me back."

When the carriage came, they boarded and told the driver to take them to their hotel.

Chapter Twenty-Four

As they entered their hotel Clarice asked, “Did you see anything back there?”

“Nothing around the theater,” Clint said. “No one seems very interested in it.”

Hopefully, that will change tomorrow night when I start singing,” she said.

Clint walked her to the door of her suite.

“What will you be doing?” she asked.

“I’ll be in my room, cleaning my weapons,” Clint said.

“Are you expecting trouble?” she asked.

“I always keep my weapons clean and ready,” Clint told her. “That’s what you’re paying me for.”

She frowned.

“Am I paying you?”

“Room and board will do,” he said. “Also, a nice meal or two.”

She went into her suite, and he walked down the hall to his room.

***

Clint worked diligently on his Peacemaker, his rifle and his New Line, cleaning them thoroughly. His gun had recently jammed on him, the first and only time it had ever happened. He was determined that would never happen again.

He hoped that, in traveling with Clarice, he wouldn't have to use his guns. Unfortunately, as long as he was the Gunsmith—and he would always be—his guns were part of his life. He could only hope that his time with Clarice would be spent in her world, not his. Music instead of guns.

Clarice and Clint had agreed to have dinner on their own on this night before her performance. For this reason he went down to the hotel dining room, since the meals they had in Clarice's suite were acceptable.

He was shown to a table in the half-empty room, which allowed him to sit alone. His meal was pleasant and uninterrupted. While he was eating a slice of peach pie and washing it down with coffee, he was surprised to see Rebecca walk into the dining room. She headed right for his table, as if she knew he would be there.

"Well, well," he said, as she reached him.

"Mind if I join you for dessert?" she asked.

"Please do."

She sat across from him.

"This won't get you in trouble with Clarice, will it?"

"She's eating in her room," Clint said. "She won't be down here."

The waiter came over and she said, "I'll have what he's having."

"Yes, Ma'am."

"What's on your mind, Rebecca?" he asked. "You interviewed Clarice on the train, and you're going to review her performance tomorrow."

"Yes, but I'm interested in the rest of her tour. Where she's going from here, and so on."

"I'm afraid that's between her and me," Clint said.

"What are you worried about?" Rebecca asked. "Somebody getting there before you?"

"This is just the way we planned it," he said. "Sorry."

The waiter brought her pie and coffee.

"Oh well," she said, "at least I get a slice of pie out of it."

"Yes, you do."

"Unless . . ."

"Unless what?" he asked.

"We never did get to finish what we started on the train," she said. "You know, under the blanket."

"No, we didn't," Clint said.

"So what do you say?" she asked. "After the pie you can show me your room."

He smiled.

"Why not?"

***

When they entered his room they wasted no time taking their clothes off then racing to the bed. He enjoyed watching every jiggle and jump of her fleshy body as she ran ahead of him.

She leaped on the bed ahead of him and turned on her butt, opening her legs wide to show him the beauty at the apex of her thighs. On the train he had his fingers in there, but this was the first time he was seeing it.

Putting a hand on each thigh he drove his face into her wetness, and put his tongue and lips to work on her.

“Ooooh Goood,” she moaned, gripping his head to hold him there—not that it was necessary. The taste and smell of her was enough to hold him.

He released her thighs and slid his hands beneath her to cup her buttocks firmly. He held her that way and continued his oral ministrations until she trembled and screamed . . .

Chapter Twenty-Five

"Oh my God," Rebecca said.

"I agree," Clint said.

They were laying side-by-side, naked and glistening with perspiration. They had been on the bed together for hours, devouring each other, and now they lay resting.

Clint turned his head to look at Rebecca. He ran his eyes up and down her bountiful body, with full breasts and hips.

"You're amazing, you know," he told her. "And beautiful."

"I was thinking the same thing about you," she said. "You're a beautiful man. I knew that even when I was stroking you under the blanket on the train. And now that I see you . . ."

He rolled over, grabbed her, pulled her to him and kissed her, while their bodies pressed together.

Breathless, she asked, "Is that your way of telling me to shut up?"

"Let's just take a little rest," he suggested, releasing her. "There's much of the night left."

"Sounds good to me," she said.

They closed their eyes, and both drifted off . . .

***

When they woke, it was early light.

Rebecca turned to Clint and punched him in the shoulder, waking him.

"We slept the rest of the night!" she complained.

Clint stretched, yawned and said, "We needed it."

She fell into the sheets on her back and said, "Yeah, I guess we did."

He rolled toward her, ran his hand down her body and said, "But we still have the morning."

"Mmmmm," she hummed, turning toward him . . .

***

After a heated session that lasted forty minutes, they each rolled to their side of the bed and put their feet on the floor.

"A bath?" she asked.

"You have your own hotel, don't you?"

"Yes, a few streets away."

"Then I say breakfast first, then you can worry about a bath."

"Agreed."

"So we wash up, get dressed and go down to the dining room," he said.

"Sounds like a plan," She stood up and walked to the mirror. "Oh God, my hair!"

***

They made it to the dining room while it was still mostly empty. The waiter greeted and seated them, and fetched their order.

While they were eating Rebecca said, "How about a favor?"

"Ask and we'll see."

"Ask Clarice if you can give me her tour schedule," she said.

"You're going to review her performance this evening," Clint said. "Why go any further? She's going to be touring for weeks."

"It sounds like more fun than sitting home waiting for something else to review," Rebecca said.

"Well," Clint said, "I can ask her, but she seems to want fresh ears at every performance."

"Never hurts to ask," Rebecca said. "If she says no, I'll have to head for home tomorrow. We'll probably never see each other again."

"Then our last night will be memorable."

"There's no way you'd ever be a one woman man, is there?" she asked.

"I'm afraid not."

"Too bad," Clarice said. "Guess I'll see you at the theater tonight.

"I'll have your answer by then," he told her.

She left and he went to his room.

***

Later, he dressed for the theater and went to Clarice's suite to pick her up. When she opened the door, she was radiant in a floor length green gown with exposed, creamy white shoulders.

"Ready?" he asked.

"I'm always ready," she said.

As they walked to the front door she said, "This will be the first time you hear me sing."

"Yes, it will."

"I hope you enjoy it."

As they reached the door he said, "I'm sure I will."

Chapter Twenty-Six

She sang like an angel.

Starke arranged for Clint to stand backstage during the performance, but he couldn't imagine Clarice would have sounded better if he was in the front row.

Everything seemed to be going well, and when the last song finished, Clint waited for Clarice to come off stage. He was surprised that when she did it was on the dead run, frantically.

"It's him! He's here!" she cried, grabbing his arms.

"Hey, take it easy," he said. "Who's here?"

"The glaring man," she said. "He was right there in the front row, glaring at me like he wanted me dead!"

"Stay here!" Clint snapped.

The crowd was already moving toward the exits. The only way he thought he might catch the man was to get to the exit first. Luckily, his visit to the theater the day before showed him a way to do that. Unfortunately, even though he got outside fast, some of the crowd had already exited. But Clarice said the man had been in the front row. That meant he would be one of the last to get to the exit.

He had Clarice's description of the man but wasn't seeing anyone who matched it. Eventually, the crowd thinned out and he knew the man had gotten away.

He went back inside to Clarice's dressing room. When he knocked she asked, "Who is it?"

"Clint."

She opened the door with a worried look on her face.

"Did you get him?"

"No," Clint said, "I didn't see anyone matching the description you gave me."

"You should have kept looking!"

"There was a huge crowd out there," Clint said. "He could have easily faded away. Are you sure it was him?"

"I'm positive," she said.

"What did he do?"

"He just . . . glared at me."

There was a knock at the door. Clint waved Clarice back and went to the door. He cracked it, then opened it wide to admit Mr. Starke.

"My dear," he said, "you were spectacular."

"Thank you," she said.

"Especially the last song," he said. "It was amazing."

Clint wondered if that had anything to do with her seeing the glaring man in the audience. Perhaps that added some intensity to her performance.

***

When they got back to the hotel, Clint went to Clarice's suite with her.

Clarice stormed in and tossed her wrap down on the sofa.

"He followed us here!" she screamed. "How did he do that?"

"There's another possibility," Clint said.

She whirled on him, hands on hips.

"What's that?"

"Somehow, he got ahold of your schedule."

"And how could he have done that?"

"I don't know," Clint said, "any more than I know how he could have followed us. I'd swear he wasn't on that train with us."

"I don't know if I can go on tomorrow night."

"You agreed to two nights, right?"

"Yes."

"Then I think you have to go on," Clint said. "You have to keep your word, and it may be our only chance to catch him."

"And if we don't catch him, he'll follow us to our next stop."

"Eventually, he'll make a mistake."

"And if he doesn't?"

"So far he hasn't done anything but watch you."

"Glare at me!" she corrected.

"Okay, glare at you," Clint agreed, "but he hasn't tried to hurt you."

"And I don't want to wait for that," she said.

"Then go on tomorrow night as planned, and I'll see if I can catch him."

"How will you do that?"

"I can ask the local police for help," Clint said. "With a few of their men we could cover the entire theater."

"Do you think they'd do that?"

"I think I can ask," Clint said. "That's a start."

She stared at him.

"What would your manager tell you to do?"

She compressed her lips, flared her nostrils, and said, "He would tell me to go on."

"So then what are we going to do?"

"I'll go on," she said, tightly "and you do what you have to do."

Okay," Clint said. "You have dinner and get some rest, and I'll go and see the local law."

Chapter Twenty-Seven

Clint made his way, by carriage, to the local police station. Like most modern police stations in the East, and several that had appeared in the West, there was a front desk with one uniformed officer stationed at it.

"Can I help you, sir?" the young officer asked.

"I need to speak to someone in authority."

The young man frowned.

"You really shouldn't be wearing a gun into this building, sir."

"I can explain that to whoever's in charge."

"I'll need your name, sir."

"My name is Clint Adams."

The man looked surprised.

"Excuse me, sir, is that Clint Adams . . . the Gunsmith?" he asked.

"That's right."

"I guess I can see why you're wearing your gun," the officer said. "Let me get someone to come out and talk to you. Have a seat."

"Thank you."

The young man left his position and walked further into the building. Clint sat on a wooden bench by the front door.

The young officer reappeared with an older, stocky, grey-haired man in a long-sleeved white shirt and suspenders.

"Mr. Adams," he said, approaching Clint. "I understand you need to speak to someone in authority. How much authority are we talking about?"

"I'd like to borrow some of your men," Clint said. "Do you have the authority to grant that request?"

"I hold the rank of Captain," He said, "so I probably do. But why would I?"

"Can we go someplace and talk about it?"

"We can," the man said. "My name is Captain Ames. Come with me."

He led Clint down a hall to an office, where they sat across a desk from each other.

"Very well," Ames said. "What's this about?"

"Have you heard of Clarice DuPont?"

"She's a singer, in town to perform at our theater."

"Good, that makes it easier." He told Ames about the glaring man who had apparently followed him and Clarice from New York.

"Wait," Ames said, "all he's done is look at her?"

"So far," Clint said, "but he's managed to do it in a threatening manner."

"So what do you want to do with my men?"

"I'll position them around the theater, at all the exits. Hopefully, one of them will spot this man."

"How will they know him?" Ames asked.

"We'll describe him well."

Ames sat back in his chair and thought a moment.

"How many men would you need?"

"Perhaps . . . half a dozen."

"In uniform?"

"I think civilian clothes would be better. That way our man won't be warned."

"So we don't know whether or not he's armed?"

"No, we don't," Clint said, "but I think we should assume he is."

Ames took another moment to think.

"Do you need to get anyone's permission for this?" Clint asked.

"No, I think I can make this decision myself," Ames said. "You can have your men, but there'll be seven."

"Seven?"

"Yes," Ames said, "I have tickets for tomorrow night's performance for me and my wife."

***

Clint went back to the hotel and knocked on the door of Clarice's suite. Her dinner cart had been wheeled out into the hall.

When she opened the door he said, "I managed to get six local policemen for tomorrow night. They'll be watching all the exits."

"That's good," she said.

"I'll need you to give them a description of the man," Clint went on.

"I can do that."

"Good," Clint said. "We'll meet with them in your dressing room."

"That suits me," she said. "Are you going to tell Mr. Starke about this?"

"No," he said, "I want to keep this between us."

"That suits me, too," she said.

"Get a good night's sleep," he said. "Tomorrow should be a big day."

Chapter Twenty-Eight

The next night Clint and Clarice met with Captain Ames and his men in her dressing room.

"Okay," Clint said, "you've all been given exit doors to cover."

"Miss DuPont will describe the man to you," Ames said. "If you see him going in or coming out, grab him."

"Arrest him?" one officer asked.

"Just hold him and contact me or Mr. Adams," Ames said.

"Yessir."

Clarice launched into a detailed description of her glaring man.

"Admirably done," Ames said. "All right, you men take your positions."

"Yessir," they all said, and left the dressing room. Clint, Clarice, and Ames remained.

"I have to stay here until Mr. Starke comes for me," Clarice said.

"Then we'll take our positions," Clint said. "The Captain will go and sit with his wife. I'll go backstage. If you see the man, Clarice, don't hesitate. Point him out."

"Right."

Clint and Ames left the dressing room.

***

Clint took up his position backstage. From there he could see Clarice, the band, and the front rows, where Ames and his wife were seated.

Starke and Clarice came from her dressing room. The band leader joined his musicians. Clarice stood next to Clint, waiting for her introduction.

"Good luck," he said.

"You've heard me sing," she said. "I don't need luck. You just catch that man."

"Is he in the front row yet?"

"She craned her neck to look.

"No."

"All right," Clint said, "let's see if he tries to get in and out one of the doors."

Starke's voice announced, "Ladies and gentlemen, Miss Clarice DuPont."

Clarice walked out on stage to loud applause. The music started, and she sang. Clint listened, but his eyes continued to scan the crowd.

Clarice had four songs to sing. Clint was no expert, but it sounded like she was doing it beautifully, despite the tension she must be feeling.

Apparently, by the fourth song, she still hadn't spotted the glaring man. There were no reports from Ames' men that any of them had seen him. Clint was starting to wonder if Clarice had really seen him the night before, or simply imagined it.

When the performance ended, Clarice left the stage to thunderous applause.

"What happened?" she demanded.

"What do you mean? Did you see him?"

"No, but he must've been out there."

"I'll check with Ames and his men," Clint said. "Meanwhile, you lock yourself in your dressing room."

She went to do that while Clint went to meet with Captain Ames. He found the man out in front of the theater, looking concerned. A carriage was pulling away from the theater.

"What happened?" Clint asked.

"I just sent one of my men to the hospital," Ames said. "He was found unconscious at his post. Somebody hit him over the head."

"I'm sorry to hear that," Clint said. "We don't know if our man did it going in, or sneaking out."

"No."

"Clarice didn't see him in the theater."

"And none of my men saw anyone matching her description," Ames said. "I'm afraid we weren't very much help to you, Mr. Adams."

"Don't take it so hard," Clint said. "This fella apparently knows what he's doing. I'm probably going to have to deal with him further along on this tour."

"Unless . . ."

"Unless what?"

"Unless the lady's wrong, and he doesn't exist."

"Then who knocked out your man?"

"Good point," Ames said. "You and the lady will be leaving town tomorrow?"

"Early train."

"Would you want some of my men to escort you to the station?"

"I don't think so," Clint said. "This man seems to do all of his glaring in theaters."

"Then I guess we won't see each other again." Ames put his hand out. "It was nice meeting you. You're not at all what I would have expected."

Clint shook the captain's hand.

"Please tell the lady my wife and I enjoyed her performance."

"Will do, Captain. And thanks."

Clint watched the captain walk away, then went back inside.

Chapter Twenty-Nine

Abilene

The next stop on the tour was Chicago. After that they would work their way south to St. Louis and Kansas City, and then head west.

The theaters Clarice played became less and less fancy, but her performances were well attended, and went off beautifully. They were put up in fine hotels and fed well.

They made their way to Abilene, Kansas without another sighting of the glaring man. While Abilene was no longer a major hub for shipping cattle east, it was a major stop for travelers, and boasted many hotels and a major theater, which had booked Clarice DuPont for two nights.

Clint and Clarice disembarked from the Atchison, Topeka and Sante Fe Railroad car in Abilene and were taken to the Abilene House Hotel by a carriage that had been sent for them.

"So much dust," Clarice complained, fanning her face.

"I told you once we got West it'd be a bit more rustic," Clint said.

"You said rustic," she said, "You didn't say we'd be in a dust bowl. Is it going to get worse than this?"

"Denver's more modern," he said. "You'll like it there, and that's your next to last stop."

"Before Tombstone," she said.

"Why did your manager book Tombstone?" Clint wondered.

"He heard of The Birdcage Theater and wanted me to play it," she said. "I allowed him to make all my arrangements."

"I could cancel it," Clint said.

"Why?"

"It's a long way south from Denver," Clint said, "and the theater caters more to drinkers and gamblers. It's a tough town."

"I've heard of the O.K. Corral shootout," she said.

"That's only part of it."

"Is it tougher than Abilene?"

"A lot tougher."

"I'll give it some thought."

When they got to the hotel, a few men grabbed their bags and brought them in while Clint registered them at the desk.

"Miss DuPont has our largest room," the clerk said.

“A suite?” she asked.

“I’m sorry, Ma’am, we don’t have suites,” he said, handing Clint the keys.

A man carrying her bags dropped one and she said, “And not very good bell boys.”

“They ain’t bellboys, Ma’am,” the clerk said, “they just carry bags for us.”

“Is there a bathtub in the room?” she asked.

“I’m sorry, we don’t have indoor plumbing. But there are tubs down here. Would you like me to have a bath drawn for you?”

“Yes,” she said. “A hot one.”

“Yes, Ma’am.”

Clint walked Clarice to her room, which while large, was small and plain compared to what she was used to.

“My God,” she said.

“It’s going to be this way until Denver,” he told her.

She sat on the small sofa.

“Will you take me downstairs for my bath?” she asked. “I don’t think I want to go alone.”

“Whenever you’re ready,” he said. “My room’s down the hall. I’m just going to freshen up.”

“With what?” she asked.

He pointed to the top of the dresser against the wall. “Pitcher-and-basin.”

He left and walked to his own room. It was smaller still, but it was something he was used to, traveling through the West as he did.

Using the pitcher-and-basin in the room he washed off the travel dust and donned a new shirt. As he had done during all their other stops, he planned on checking out the theater, keeping an eye out for Clarice's glaring man.

Apparently, if he was following, he had been staying out of sight after Pittsburgh. Or he had stopped attending her performances altogether. That last would have been preferable. But first he would take Clarice down for her bath.

He walked up the hall to her door and knocked. She answered, wearing a robe.

"Ready?" he asked.

"As I'll ever be," she said. "I assume they'll supply soap and towels."

"I have no doubt," Clint said.

They went down to the front desk, where the clerk handed Clarice a folded towel with a bar of soap on top of it.

"Down that hall you'll find three small rooms. Room two has your hot bath, Ma'am."

"Thank you."

Clint and Clarice walked down the hall to the door of room two.

"Are you coming in?" she asked.

"I'll keep an eye out here," he told her. "Take as long as you need."

She nodded and went inside.

Chapter Thirty

Clint stationed himself outside Clarice's bath door. Before long he could hear her moving about in the water. She was in there twenty minutes when two men wearing side arms, carrying a towel and soap bars, came down the hall. They were both in their thirties and looked like they had been riding hard.

"Hello, friend," one of them said.

"Hello."

"You must be guarding somethin' pretty special behind that door."

"Just seeing to it that a lady has privacy."

"One and three are open?" the other man asked.

"Yup."

"Wouldn't mind havin' ya guard our doors, so we know we'll be safe," the first man said.

"I'll be here until the lady's finished," Clint said. "After that you'll be on your own."

"That's okay," the second man said. "We wuz just kiddin'. We been ridin' for days, so we're gonna soak for a while."

"Well," Clint said, "enjoy your soak."

"Much obliged," the first man said. He went through door one, while his partner went into room three. Clint remained at his station, arms folded.

***

Inside the bathroom Clarice could see that the three rooms were not all isolated. The walls between did not extend to the ceiling, as they were erected to make three small rooms out of one big one.

She heard the doors to the other rooms open and someone step in, heard them filling the tubs with water while she sat there and washed. She didn't expect trouble, but she kept looking both ways as she washed.

***

The two men were brothers, Ab and Seth Musgrave. They had been paid to do a job, and it seemed to be a fairly simple one.

They filled the tubs with buckets of water, but never took off their clothes. They each moved a chair over to the temporary wall so they could step up, and peer over at the naked lady in the tub.

"Well, lookee there, Ab," Seth, the younger brother said, "ain't she pretty?"

"She surely is, Seth," Ab agreed.

Clarice caught her breath, crossed her arms over her breasts, and shouted, "Clint!"

***

Clint heard Clarice, turned and burst into the room. He saw Clarice sitting in the tub with her arms crossed. He heard running footsteps out in the hall.

"Two men were looking at me over these walls," Clarice said.

"Just stay in here. I'll be right back," he said, and ran out the door.

There was nobody in the hall, but he knew they had run toward the front desk, so he ran that way. When he came out into the lobby, there was no one there but the desk clerk.

"Where'd they go?" Clint asked.

"You mean the Musgrave Brothers?" the clerk asked. "I thought they were takin' baths, but they ran out of here pretty quick."

"Which way?"

"They went out the front door."

Clint ran to the front door and looked out at the street. There was no sign of the two men. He went back to the desk.

"What's your name?" Clint asked.

"Jeremy," the young man said.

"You mentioned the Musgrave Brothers. Tell me about them."

"They're locals, they do odd jobs for people."

"They live around here?"

"Outside of town somewhere, I ain't sure where."

"I saw them wearing guns," Clint said. "Do they hire them out?"

Jeremy shrugged.

"Pretty much anythin' people want, they do."

"And they said they were going to take baths?"

"Yup," Jeremy said, "I gave them towels and soap, but I thought it was odd. They never did that here before."

"Did they ask about the lady?"

"No, sir."

"Okay," Clint said, "thanks."

He went back down the hall to Clarice. He knocked on the door.

"You decent?"

"Come in."

He entered, found her seated in a chair, wearing her robe and drying her hair.

"Who were they?" she asked.

"A couple of locals who hire out."

"So somebody hired them to do that?" she asked.

"Seems like it."

She pursed her lips and said, "It was him."

"The glaring man?"

She nodded.

"But he's still around."

"That remains to be seen," Clint said. "Right now, let's get you up to your room."

Chapter Thirty-One

Clint walked Clarice to her room, made sure she was locked inside, then left to check the security at the theater.

"I'll be as fast as I can," Clint said. "Meanwhile, I can leave you this." He held out his Colt New Line. She accepted it.

"Do you know how to use that?" he asked.

"I've never fired a gun before," she said, "but it doesn't seem very difficult."

"True," Clint said. "Just point and pull the trigger."

"All right."

"You'll want to hit your target here," he said, circling his chest with his hand.

"I don't want to kill anybody."

"You'll only use this if somebody's trying to hurt you," Clint told her. "What if it's your glaring man?"

She set her jaw and said, "Then I'll kill him. He probably killed Leo."

"That's true." He went to the door. "I'll be back soon, and I'll bring food."

"Sounds good," she said.

He stepped out, closed the door and waited to hear her lock it before leaving.

***

The Abilene Theater was rather small, with only one way in and out. Clint entered, saw a group of musicians on the stage, laughing with each other. He walked down the middle aisle. When they saw him they all turned and watched.

"My name's Clint Adams," he said. "I'm here representing Clarice DuPont."

"Ah, the songbird we're waitin' for," one of the men said. "You must be lookin' for our bandleader. He's in the back. I'll show ya."

The musician dropped down from the stage and led Clint to a backstage door.

"Our boss's name is Harry Page, he's back here goin' over the song list. Is the lady comin' in today?"

"She'll be here early tomorrow," Clint said. "I'm checking on security today."

"Security?" the man said. "You lookin' for trouble?"

"Hopefully not."

"The boss is back here."

He led Clint to a backstage area where a man was seated at a desk, studying some papers.

"Boss, Mr. Adams is here. He represents the song lady."

Harry Page turned and looked at Clint. He was fiftyish, tall, lean, and rough looking, more like a rancher than a theater bandleader.

"Mr. Adams," he said, extending his hand, "great to meet you."

"Mr. Page."

"Oh, call me Harry," the man said. "Everybody does. Is Miss DuPont with you?"

"I'll bring her here tomorrow morning to go over the performance with you. As I told this gent, I'm here about security."

"Well," Page said, one way in and one way out, that's about it. What kind of trouble are you looking for?"

"Miss DuPont's being followed by a man," Clint said, "We're on the lookout for him."

"Well," Page said, "give us a description and we'll all look for him. Our audiences aren't that big, but we're hopin' for the best for Miss DuPont."

"I'll do that," Clint said. "What about the local law?"

"We've got Sheriff Lou Harper, he's been wearing our Abilene star for a few years. He ain't a theater goer, but he'll be happy to help, I'm sure."

"Then I should drop by and see him," Clint said.

"I'll have Eddie, here, walk ya over to his office," Page said. "As for tomorrow mornin', I'll meet you and the lady right here."

"Good," Clint said, shaking the man's hand again. "Much thanks."

***

Eddie led Clint from the little theater down Abilene's main street to the sheriff's office. Walking the streets of Abilene made Clint feel right at home after his visits to some of the larger theaters on the tour.

"Want me to come in with you and introduce ya?" Eddie asked.

"That's not necessary," Clint said. "I think the sheriff and I will get along."

"Then I'll see you and the songbird lady tomorrow?" Eddie asked.

The musician headed back to the theater while Clint mounted the boardwalk and approached the front door to the sheriff's office.

Chapter Thirty-Two

As Clint entered the office a man was coming out from the cell block, carrying a broom. He was average height. In his sixties, with a bushy white mustache. He had a huge chew of tobacco in one cheek.

"Hello, there," he said. "Help ya?"

"Are you Sheriff Lou Harper?" Clint asked.

The man laughed.

"Sheriff and swamper," he said, setting the broom aside. "Who would you be?"

"My name's Clint Adams," Clint said. "I'm here with Clarice DuPont, who's going to sing in your Abilene Theater."

"Ah, I heard about that," Harper said. "That theater ain't someplace I go. Saloon's more my meat. What-all can I do fer ya?"

"We've got a man who's been following us since New York," Clint explained, "I want to make sure he doesn't get into the theater."

"Ya want me to stand watch?"

"You're the local law."

"Then I'll be there," the sheriff said. "Just tell me when."

"Two nights from now, seven sharp," Clint said. "She goes on at eight."

"I'll be there."

"Just like that?" Clint asked.

"Why not?" the sheriff asked, with a shrug. "I ain't got nothin' else to do. In fact, I got nothin' to do now. Why don't we go across to the Alhambra and get a beer?"

"Sounds good to me," Clint said. "Let's go"

***

The sheriff led Clint across the street to the saloon which, at that time of day, was mostly empty. They bellied up to the bar and the bartender came over.

"Hey, Sheriff," the big man said, "who's yer friend?"

"Mike," Sheriff Harper said, "meet Clint Adams."

"The Gunsmith?" Mike blurted. "Welcome to Abilene."

"Thanks, Mike."

"What can I get you fellas?"

"Two beers," Harper said.

"Comin' up."

The Alhambra had a large interior, with at least half a dozen gaming tables, currently covered with tarps.

They both picked up their beers, turned their backs and leaned against the bar.

"Faro, blackjack, craps and roulette," Harper said. "They pull the tarps off after six."

"What about poker?"

"No house games, but a couple of games usually pop up," Harper said.

"Tell me about a couple of brothers called Musgrave." Clint said.

"Ab and Seth," Harper said. "You met them?"

"Briefly."

"A couple of local troublemakers," the lawman said. "Somebody usually pays them to cause trouble."

"Who pays them?" Clint asked. "Do they work for one person?"

"They work for anybody who'll pay them," Harper said.

"How far will they go?" Clint asked.

"That depends on who's payin'," Harper said, "and how much. How far did they go with you?"

"Not very," Clint said, "but I'd still like to find them."

"Well, they live outside of town, but nobody really knows where."

"Then how do people find them to hire them?"

"They're usually in one saloon or another," Harper said. "Do you wanna look for them?"

Clint sipped his beer and thought. His responsibility was Clarice and her performance.

"No," he said, finally. "I need to get back to my hotel and Miss DuPont. Tomorrow morning I'll take her to the theater to set up her performance."

"Okay, then," Harper said. "I'll meet you in front of the theater the mornin' of her performance."

"Good," Clint said. "I think you'll like her singing."

"Oh, I ain't gonna go inside," the older man said. "I toldja, theater ain't fer me. But I'll make sure she's safe inside, and gets to show."

"That's good enough for me," Clint said.

He paid for the beers, shook hands with Sheriff Harper, gave Mike a salute, and left the Alhambra.

"Is he here to kill somebody, Sheriff?" the bartender asked.

"What makes you ask that, Mike?" Harper replied.

"Well," the bartender said, "he is the Gunsmith. Ain't that what he does?"

"You're talkin' about a reputation," Harper said, "not a man."

"Some reputations are deserved," Mike pointed out.

"Then I guess we'll find out about this one."

Chapter Thirty-Three

When Clint returned to the hotel he did so with a tray of food for Clarice that he purchased at a nearby café. He bought enough for both of them, so they sat together, ate and talked.

"What did you find out?" she asked.

"The theater is small, with only one door. I've arranged for the sheriff to be on the door the day of your performance. Tomorrow I'll take you over to meet the bandleader."

"What about the two men this morning?"

"Apparently, they're a couple of brothers named Musgrave. They hire out for odd jobs."

"You mean someone hired them to peek at me in the bathtub?" she said. "I wonder who that could have been."

"So we can assume your glaring man is here," Clint surmised.

"Who else?" she replied.

"You're probably right."

"You know," she said, "with your reputation, I assumed you'd be able to catch this fellow."

"I still have time," he told her. "I certainly don't want to disappoint you."

"I don't mean to criticize you," she said, "but I don't want to return home with this thing unresolved."

"I can't blame you for that," he said. "I could go looking for these Musgrave Brothers to find out who hired them, but they're local and could easily hide. And we have a few more stops on this tour before we hit Tombstone and the Birdcage. I have a feeling to end this at the Birdcage might be this glaring man's plan. I mean, if he's been dragging this out all this time, he must have an end in mind."

"So are you suggesting we don't go to the Bird-cage?" she asked.

"No," Clint said, "I'm suggesting we just go ahead and end it there. Then you go home with peace of mind."

"Then we're agreed," she said. "But what about Denver?"

"Denver will have a very large theater," Clint said. "And I have a friend there I can press into service, if he's available. Your glaring man may very well show up there, because it would be easy for him to get lost in a crowd. I'll make every effort to catch him there, but I think this is all going to end in Tombstone."

"And you've been to Tombstone before?"

"Several times," Clint said. "It's always been a tough town."

"Why would this man choose Tombstone, then?" she asked. "It's a rough western town, and he is apparently an Easterner,"

"I can't say," Clint said. "He may be comfortable anywhere. And there's still one other thing."

"What's that?"

"He's made no move to harm you."

"He killed Leo!"

"We don't know that for sure," Clint said.

"Then who did?"

"I don't know," Clint said. "I didn't know Leo. Was he a gambler? Was he sleeping with somebody's wife?"

"On that last one I can definitely tell you no," she told him.

"Okay, but you see my point. We don't know for sure that your glaring man has done anything more than glare."

"Why would he come all this way just to do that?" she demanded. "No, he has something planned."

"So let's find out what that is," Clint said.

They finished eating and Clint piled the plates on the tray so he could return them to the café.

"Why not see if the desk clerk has someone who can do that?" Clarice suggested. "I don't really feel like being alone here."

"That's a good idea," Clint said. "I'll take these down to the lobby and come right back."

***

As Clint carried the tray down, he thought about Clarice. He hadn't realized that the Musgrave Brothers peering over the walls at her had upset her so. Up to now she had been content to lock her doors and remain in her hotel rooms, alone. Abilene had apparently changed that.

When Clint explained to the young desk clerk what he wanted, the man quickly agreed.

"Of course, sir," he said. "Just leave the tray here and I'll have it returned."

"Thank you."

Clint turned to leave but hesitated and turned back.

"Have you seen the Musgrave Brothers again?" he asked.

"No, sir."

"Has anyone else been in here looking for me or Miss DuPont?"

"No, sir, nobody."

"You'd let me know if anyone was, right?"

"I know who you are, Mr. Adams," the clerk said. "If anybody came in here looking for the Gunsmith, I'd surely let you know."

"That's good," Clint said. "I'm much obliged."

He turned and headed back to the second floor.

Chapter Thirty-Four

The next morning Clint accompanied Clarice to the theater to meet Harry Page. The bandleader was waiting in front of the theater.

"This is the theater?" Clarice asked as they approached.

"Don't be disappointed," Clint said. "They do the best they can."

"What will the Birdcage be like?"

"Slightly larger," Clint said, "but you'll still find it rustic."

"Miss DuPont," Page said, as they reached him. "How wonderful to meet you."

They shook hands.

"If we can go inside, we can go over your songs."

"That's fine," she said. "Clint?"

"I think I'll keep watch out here," Clint told her, "just in case."

"Fine," she said, then turned to Page. "Shall we?"

"By all means."

He opened the door for her, then followed her inside.

***

Clint remained out front while Clarice worked on her program with Harry Page. He noticed that very few people who strolled by the theater paid it—or him—much attention. And there was no sign of the glaring man, or the Musgrave Brothers.

He wondered how a man who came east from New York had managed to find the Musgraves and hire them. Of course, there was always the possibility that the brothers had simply spotted Clarice and decided to take a peek at the beautiful, naked woman. Clint did not have the time to actively search for them now.

As the morning turned to afternoon, he wondered how the meeting inside the theater was going. At one point, two of the musicians he had seen the day before came out the door. One of them was the man who introduced him to Page.

"Mr. Adams," the man said. "Are you waiting for Miss DuPont?"

"I am."

"She and Harry are deep in discussion about the program," the man said. "Would you like to have lunch with us?"

"I would actually, but I think I'd better stay right here for now."

"Security," the man said. "I understand."

"Enjoy your lunch," Clint said to both men.

"Thanks."

The men walked away.

***

Clint was still in place when they returned from lunch and exchanged a wave with him on the way back in. Some of the other musicians had also gone to lunch and returned. Only Clarice and Harry Page remained inside. Clint noticed one of the musicians bringing some food in which he assumed was for the songstress and the bandleader. His own stomach was growling, but he remained in place.

Finally, in late afternoon, Clarice and Page reappeared.

"How'd it go?" he asked.

"Wonderfully," Page said. "We're all set for tomorrow." Page took Clarice's hand and actually kissed it. "Until tomorrow." He went inside.

"Did he actually do that?" Clint asked.

"He's a bit of a ham. How about some food?"

"Didn't you eat? I saw someone bring food in."

"It wasn't very much."

"Then let's find a place," Clint said.

They started off down the street. Within a few blocks they encountered a likely looking café called Silver Street Café.

"This isn't Silver Street," Clarice said.

"No, it isn't, but it looks okay."

They peered in through a large, plate glass window that bore the name and saw a busy interior.

"Let's see if we can get a table," Clint said.

"Suits me."

They entered and looked around. There were several empty tables scattered about. Clint spotted one against the back wall.

"Help ya?" a waiter asked.

"That back table," Clint said.

"Nobody ever sits there," the older man said. "People like to sit among other people."

"We'll sit there," Clint said.

"Suit yerself."

He led them to the table and seated them.

"Menus?"

Clint looked around. A lot of the people seemed to be eating the same thing.

"You got a special?"

"We do."

"We'll take two."

The special turned out to be beef stew. The waiter served it with a basket of warm biscuits.

"This is delicious," Clarice said.

"Rustic but good," Clint said.

"All right, so Abilene is a little plain for my taste," she admitted. "This hotel, the theater, the streets, but this food is good."

"Wait til you meet the sheriff tomorrow," Clint said. "He's hanging onto the past."

"There's no modern police department here?"

"No," Clint said, "and there won't be one in Tombstone, either."

"What about Denver?"

"Denver is a very modern city," Clint said. "You'll feel right at home."

"I can't wait," she said.

They concentrated on their meal. By the time they finished, most of the other diners had gone.

"Dessert?" the waiter asked.

"Sure," Clarice said. "What've you got?"

"Pies."

"Peach?" she asked.

"Oh, yes."

"Bring two slices," Clint said, "and coffee."

"Comin' up."

"So what did you think of Mr. Page?" Clint asked, as the server walked away.

"A little rough-hewn," Clarice said, "but he enjoys his theater."

"And the theater?"

She shrugged.

"Like the rest of Abilene," she said. "I'll do what I can with it."

"And the musicians?"

"They'll do," she said.

"Have you ever thought about traveling with your own band?" he asked.

"That would be a very expensive proposition," she explained to him. "It's better for me if the theaters I play in supply their own music."

The waiter returned, set down the pie, two coffee cups and a pot of coffee. He poured the cups full.

"Enjoy," he said, and withdrew.

They both took a bite and found the pie to be utterly delicious. Clint thought it even better than what he'd had on the train.

When they were finished, Clint paid the bill. By the time they left, they were the last of the diners. They headed back to the hotel.

Chapter Thirty-Five

The night of the performance—and there was only going to be one night—Clint and Clarice were met at the front door by Sheriff Lou Harper.

"Nobody inside yet but musicians," the old sheriff said.

"Good," Clint said. "Sheriff Harper, meet Miss Clarice DuPont."

"A pleasure, Ma'am," Harper said. "I hope you do real good tonight."

"Thank you, Sheriff."

She and Clint entered the theater, walked down the center aisle and went backstage. There they encountered all the musicians and Harry Page.

"Are we ready?" she asked.

"All set," Page said. "Your dressing room awaits, Ma'am. I will put my musicians in place."

"Clint?" Clarice said.

"Lead the way."

She led him to a door and opened it. When they stepped in they found themselves in a small room with a dressing table, mirror and folding screen.

"Do you want me to wait outside while you dress?" he asked.

"No," she said. "I'll use that screen."

She took the bag she was carrying behind the screen with her and, minutes later, came out with her gown on. Next she sat in front of the dressing table mirror and worked on her make-up and hair. Meanwhile, the theater began to fill up.

There was a knock at the door. When Clint opened it, he saw Harry Page standing there.

"The theater's almost full," Page said. "Are we ready?"

"Clarice?" Clint said.

"Ready."

"Then I'll see you on-stage," Page said, and hurried away.

Clarice came over and stood next to Clint.

"Walk me out?"

"My pleasure."

She slid her arm through his left and they walked out to the stage together.

"Ladies and gentlemen," they heard Harry Page announce, "Miss Clarice DuPont."

Although the theater was full, the applause was not thunderous, because even at capacity it was a small place.

"Off you go," Clint said.

Clarice walked out onto the stage . . .

***

By the end of the night the applause did almost become thunderous in the small theater. Abilene may have still been a rustic Western town, but the audience appreciated Clarice's talent.

Clarice walked offstage and smiled at Clint. They went back to her dressing room.

"Didn't see him?" Clint asked.

"No sign," she said, "and that suits me just fine."

She was behind the screen, undressing, when there was a knock at the door.

"Ready?" Clint asked.

She stepped out from behind the screen in her street clothes and said, "Ready."

Clint opened the door and admitted Harry Page and a few of the musicians.

"You were wonderful!" Page gushed.

"Great!" one of the musicians said.

"Thank you," Clarice said. "You were all very good."

"The theater is emptying," Page said, "but people are raving about you on the way out."

"That's good to know," she said. "Thank you."

"Would you have a drink with us to celebrate?" Page asked.

"I'm afraid not," Clarice said. "We're catching an early train tomorrow morning. I'd like to go back to my hotel room and get some rest."

"Understandable," Page said. "Mr. Adams?"

"I'll take the lady back to her hotel," Clint said. "Tell me where you'll be, and I'll join you if I can."

"The Alhambra," Page said. "See you there."

He turned, spread his arms and herded his musicians out of the room.

"Ready to go?" Clint asked Clarice.

"Very."

When Clint and Clarice got to the front door, the theater was entirely empty. Outside they found a carriage waiting, compliments of Mr. Page. Sheriff Harper was nowhere in sight.

During the ride back, Clarice asked, "When is Denver?"

"We have two small stops between here and there," Clint said.

"Smaller than this?" she asked.

"Yes."

"Clint," she said, "I'd like to go straight to Denver."

"You want to cancel the next two performances?"

"Yes."

"That might throw your glaring man off his schedule."

She smiled and said, "I know."

Chapter Thirty-Six

Denver

Clint took Clarice from the Denver train station directly to the Denver House Hotel, where he usually stayed when he was in town. The desk clerk greeted him by name.

"Do you have two rooms available?" Clint asked. "One for me and a suite for the lady."

"Is this Miss Dupont?" the clerk asked.

"It is."

"Then of course we have a suite. I'll have her bags taken up."

"Thank you."

"They know you here," Clarice said, as they walked across the lobby.

"I come to Denver quite often, and always stay here."

"You have good taste," she said.

"The rooms are very nice, and the food is excellent," he told her. "You'll like it here."

"I like it, already," she said.

They followed the men with her bags up to her suite on the second floor. They set her bags down and filed out. Clint closed the door behind them.

"Where's your room?" Clarice asked.

"As usual, right down the hall," Clint said.

She looked around.

"Indoor plumbing?"

"You can have a nice hot bath, anytime," he told her.

"It gets better and better. What's the theater like?"

"It's huge."

"I hope I fill it."

"I'm sure you will," Clint said. "Do you want to eat in your suite? Or downstairs in the restaurant?"

"Let's go downstairs," she said. "I'm tired of hiding."

"Then let's each freshen up," Clint said, "and I'll pick you up in a couple of hours."

"Agreed."

"But you still have to lock the door."

"Right."

He stepped out, waited to hear the lock, then walked down the hall to his own room.

***

When he knocked on Clarice's door she answered, dressed for a night out.

"Ready?" he asked.

"Ready, and hungry."

They went down to the lobby and walked across to the dining room. The Maître d' showed them an isolated table, one that Clint usually sat at.

Clint ordered two steak dinners, wine for Clarice and beer for himself. They drank while they waited for their food.

"Do you think we've lost him by skipping two performances?" she asked.

"If he's smart," Clint said, "he'll just go to Tombstone and wait for us there."

"I'm not sure he's smart," Clarice said. "The way he glares at me always makes me think he's crazy."

"Sometimes crazy and smart go together," Clint said.

"What if he's insane?"

"That's another thing, entirely."

The waiter brought their plates and they began to eat. He topped off their drinks.

"I have to say," Clarice said, "this is better than eating in my suite."

Clint looked around the room while they ate. He didn't see anyone paying special attention to the two of them. Everyone seemed to be occupied by their own meals and dining companions.

The Denver House's restaurant usually catered to Denver's elite, and they were usually quite self-absorbed.

"What do you see?" Clarice asked.

"Nothing," Clint said. "No one is paying any attention to us."

"That's a good thing," she said. "I want all attention on me when I'm performing, not tonight."

"Well, you'll get it."

"Which theater am I playing?" she asked.

"Your manager booked you into the Oriental Theater," Clint told her. "It's very well known."

"When do I see it?"

"I think we'll both go over there tomorrow to check security and meet the bandleader."

"Good," she said. "I'm tired of staying in my suite. Maybe if I'm on the street the glaring man will come after me and you can deal with him."

"If and when he puts in an appearance, I'll do my best to deal with him," Clint told her. "Personally, I'd rather have it happen in Tombstone than here in Denver."

"Why's that?"

"There'll be less places for him to hide," Clint explained to her.

Chapter Thirty-Seven

When they reached the theater the next morning, Clarice was impressed.

"This is huge," she said. "Are you going to bring the local law into this?"

"This theater has its own security force," Clint said. "They'll cover every door. You just have to describe the glaring man."

"Right."

"But for now, let's meet your band leader."

They went inside, walked down a side aisle until they reached the stage. From there they went backstage. They found a tall man waiting for them, hands clasped behind his back.

"Miss DuPont? Mr. Adams?"

"That's right," Clint said.

"I am Leonard Harwood," the man said. "I manage this theater and the band."

"It's a pleasure to meet you, sir," Clarice said.

"We can discuss your program in my dressing room," Harwood said. "Mr. Adams, my security chief is at your disposal. He will be here shortly."

"Very good"

"Madam?"

"I'll see you later, Clint," Clarice said.

"I'll be here the whole time," Clint assured her.

Clarice allowed Harwood to escort her to his dressing room. Clint remained where he was. Five minutes later a man approached him.

"Mr. Adams?"

"That's right."

"My name's Tom Bennett, I'm Chief of Security for the Oriental."

Clint shook the man's hand. It was a surprisingly firm grip from a man barely five-and-a-half feet tall.

"If you're interested in my qualifications, I spent ten years with the Pinkertons."

"That's good enough for me."

"Can I show you around?"

"Lead the way."

"I will have a man on every door," Bennett said, as they walked . . .

***

Bennett showed Clint to every entrance and exit, introduced him to each man positioned there.

"When the lady gives us the description on this man you're looking for, we'll be all set," Bennett said. "We might as well head backstage again."

"This place is impressive," Clint said, as they walked.

"Wait til tomorrow night, when every seat is full," Bennett told him.

"Will every seat be full?" Clint asked.

"Oh, yeah," Bennett said. "Every ticket is sold. The lady is gonna pack 'em in."

"That's good to know."

"In fact," Bennett said. "I think Mr. Harwood is gonna ask her to add a night. Is that possible?"

"I don't know," Clint said. "We're on a tight schedule. We need to be in Tombstone next week."

"Tombstone?" Bennett said. "Does that still exit? I thought it was a ghost town, by now."

"Nope, it's still there, and it's still wild."

"And the Earps?"

"They've moved on."

"That whole O.K. Corral thing," Bennett asked, "was that on the level?"

"Oh yeah," Clint said, "it really happened."

"Were you there?"

"Not for the shootout," Clint said.

***

When they reached the backstage, they found Clarice and Harwood standing there, in discussion.

"Everything worked out?" Clint asked.

"We're all set," Hardwood said. "Tomorrow night will go off without a hitch."

Clarice didn't comment.

"Then I suppose we're done here," Clint said. "We'll see you tomorrow."

"I'm looking forward to it. Bennett will walk you out," Harwood said.

"This way, folks," the security chief said.

They followed him to the front door.

"Mr. Adams," Bennett said, "Ma'am, real pleased to meet you."

The security man turned and went back inside.

"I didn't give them the glaring man's description," Clarice pointed out.

"We can do that tomorrow," Clint said. "For now, let's get back to the Denver House."

Chapter Thirty-Eight

That morning, before leaving the hotel, Clint had the desk clerk send a message to his friend, Talbot Roper. He wanted to see if Roper was in town.

He and Clarice stopped at the desk to pick up any reply.

"Sorry, Mr. Adams," the clerk said. "The word we got is that Mr. Roper is out of town."

"Okay, thanks."

"Roper?" Clarice asked, as they walked to the stairs.

"A friend of mine," Clint said. "When we're in town at the same time, we get together."

"Too bad," she said. "He could have heard me sing."

"Yes," Clint said, "he could have."

Clint walked Clarice to her suite.

"Would you like to come in?" she asked. "It's been a while."

"I don't think so," Clint said. "Let's keep this all business, until after Tombstone."

Clarice did not look pleased at this suggestion, but went along with it.

"Did you keep it business with your friend Rebecca?" she asked.

"Hey," he said, "we never did read any of her reviews, did we?"

"That's because we don't know what newspapers carry her column," Clarice said. "And don't think I didn't notice you avoiding the question."

He went down the hall to his own room, still not answering her question.

***

The performance the next night at the Oriental Theater went off without a hitch. The musicians, bandleader and Clarice were treated to rousing applause. Afterward, the security chief, Bennett, reported no sightings of the glaring man. Clint doubted the man had given up. He expected they would be seeing him in Tombstone for the final performance on the tour, at the Birdcage Theater.

Clint and Clarice agreed to a glass of champagne with Mr. Harwood in his dressing room. They disappointed the man by not agreeing to a second performance the next night. They needed to be on an early train. They all shook hands, and Clint and Clarice went back to the Denver House.

Clint left Clarice in her suite, and they agreed that he would pick her up early in the morning, with men supplied by the hotel to collect her luggage.

In his room he sat in a chair and gave the rest of their trip some thought. Tombstone was the final stop. He didn't know why Delaware had set it up that way. The town's best days were certainly behind it.

Although Clint himself had never laid eyes on the glaring man, he had to admit that he felt the man's presence, even when he wasn't there. If the man had anything in mind, it seemed obvious Tombstone would be the place to bring things to a close. He didn't know who the current sheriff and marshal were, but he would certainly bring one of them in on it. He doubted the glaring man would wait until he and Clarice were back in New York.

Clint wasn't sure he was going to accompany Clarice all the way back to Manhattan. It would depend on whether or not she insisted on it. Certainly, if things with the glaring man were brought to a close in Tombstone, there would be no harm in sending her back East on her own.

Before turning in, Clint packed is meager bag of belongings for the train trip to Tombstone. When that was completed, he hung his gunbelt on the bedpost, undressed and crawled between the sheets for a good night's sleep.

Chapter Thirty-Nine

Tombstone

It was a long train ride to Tombstone, and by the time they disembarked, Clarice was exhausted.

"Oh my." She said, as they waited for her bags to be collected, "so this is the famous Tombstone."

"This is the ghost of the famous Tombstone," Clint said. "But there's still plenty of trouble on every street."

"Where will we be staying?" she asked.

"The Silver Spur Hotel," Clint said. "I'm afraid your accommodations won't be as elaborate as they were in Denver."

"I didn't think they would be," she said.

"Stay here," Clint said. "I'm going to talk to the station clerk about getting your bags to the hotel."

"Right."

She chose to sit on her locked trunk and wait.

Clint went into the station and made arrangements. Before long three men appeared with a buckboard.

"Where we goin', Mister?" one man asked.

"The Silver Spur."

"Right."

The men loaded Clarice's bags on the buckboard. Clint assisted Clarice in climbing onto the seat next to the driver, then climbed aboard the back and sat among the bags.

The buckboard's trip from the train station to the Silver Spur attracted much attention as it went by. Curious stares followed it most of the way. When it reached the hotel, a small crowd had formed across the street to watch as the bags were unloaded and taken inside, followed by Clarice and Clint.

"Do those people know who you are?" Clarice asked, as they entered the lobby.

"Some might," Clint said.

"Will someone try to shoot you?" she asked.

"I never know," Clint said.

"That's no way to live."

"It's a little late to change now," Clint said. "Let's get our rooms."

They went to the front desk.

***

Across town a man entered the Last Bullet Saloon and approached the bar.

"Help ya?" the bartender asked.

"Whiskey."

"Comin' up."

The bartender poured a shot of whiskey and set it down in front of the man. He tossed it back and slammed the glass down.

"Anythin' else?" the bartender asked.

"I'm staying at the Three Aces Hotel."

"Not the best place in town," the bartender said.

"The desk clerk told me I could find what I'm looking for in this saloon."

"And what would that be?"

"I need three men who wouldn't mind killing somebody for a price," the man said.

The bartender smirked and waved his arm.

"Take your pick," he said.

The man turned and looked at the collection of men who were seated at tables, as well as standing at the bar.

"Can you give me a hint?" he asked the bartender.

"That one," he said, pointing to a man seated alone at a table. "Also that one," pointing at a man standing at the end of the bar. "And that one," indicating another man seated alone.

"What about those three?" the man asked, pointing to three men seated together.

"You don't want three men who know each other that well," the bartender said. "You want men who are only concerned with their own well-being."

"Good point," the man said. "Thanks." He started to leave, but turned back and set some money on the bar. "Let's just forget we had this talk."

"What talk?"

"Exactly."

***

He talked to the man standing at the end of the bar first.

"I just need to know who you want killed," the man said.

"His name's Clint Adams."

"I'm interested."

"What's your price?"

The man named it.

"Agreed," the man said. "I'll be getting two more men."

"Whatever you want," the gunman said. "Just let me know when."

***

He went to one of the seated men, next.

"The Gunsmith?" the man said.

"That's right."

"Am I doin' this alone?"

"I'm hiring two other men."

"Then I'm in."

"Name your price."

The man did.

"Agreed."

***

He went to the other seated man next.

"How do you want it done?" the man asked.

"That'll be up to you and the other two men I hire," the man said. "I'll tell you where and when, but how is between you three."

"Who are the other two?"

"They're in here."

The man looked around.

"Once you've agreed, I'll put the three of you together," the man said.

The gun for hire looked around again, then said, "There's nobody in here I can't work with, so I'm in."

"Then name your price . . ."

Chapter Forty

Clint took Clarice to her room, then went to his own. Within minutes there was a knock at his door. When he opened it Clarice barged in.

"That's a terrible room!" she announced.

"It's the best room in the hotel."

"Oh my," she said. "How's the food going to be?"

"That'll depend on where we eat," Clint said, "and how much things have changed since I was last here."

She sat down on the edge of his bed.

"Why did Leo book me here?" she wondered aloud.

"I've wondered the same thing," he said, sitting next to her.

She turned her head and looked at him.

"I'm going to need something while we're here," she said.

"Like what?"

"Like you," she said, "tonight. I'm going to need you to loosen me up."

"You mean—"

"You know what I mean," she said.

He thought a moment, then said, "All right."

She turned toward him.

"Tonight," he said. "For now, let's go for a walk."

"Really? In this town?"

"You want to eat?"

"Oh, yes," she said.

"Then let's go."

***

On the walk down Front Street they went past two cafes that Clint had once eaten in. Both looked as if they had seen better days.

"There," Clint said, pointing to a third. "The Mayflower. Still looks good."

It was between lunch and dinner, so there were plenty of tables. The café may have looked the same, but the waiters were different. Clint didn't know either of them.

"Sir," the waiter said, "take any table."

"One in the back."

The waiter waved them on. They seated themselves and waited. It was the middle-aged waitress who came over to serve them.

"What can I get you two?" she asked.

"I want breakfast," Clarice said. "Bacon, eggs and biscuits."

"Spuds?" the waitress asked.

“No thanks.”

“Sir?”

“You got meat loaf?”

“We do.”

“I’ll have a sandwich.”

“Comin’ up.’

From where they were seated they could still see out the front window.

“So this is Tombstone.”

“It is,” Clint said.

“Where’s the Birdcage Theater?”

"A few blocks from here,” Clint said. “I’ll walk you over there after we eat.”

“How’s the security?”

“Terrible,” Clint said. “There are plenty of doors and tunnels in and out.”

“Tunnels?”

“There’s a honeycomb of whore’s cribs underneath.”

“In a theater?”

“It’s more than a theater,” Clint said. “Much more. You’ll see.”

Chapter Forty-One

"This is it?" she asked.

They were standing in front of the Birdcage Theater. Clint pointed to the sign on top of the building.

"This is it," he affirmed.

"And it has everything you said it has?"

"Whores, gambling, whiskey, beer, and music," he said, "everything."

"My God!" she breathed.

"Do you want to see the inside?"

"Do you think the bandleader is there now?" she asked.

"Probably not," Clint said. "We're supposed to meet with him tomorrow morning."

"Then let's wait til then," she said. "Who knows who's in there now?"

"That's true."

"Let's go back to our hotel," she said.

"Okay."

They walked back to the Silver Spur and went to her room, rather than Clint's.

"If anyone knows I'm here, we're safer in your room," he said.

"But if the glaring man's here, he'll come to my room."

"If he does, I'll take care of him," Clint said. "But from everything you've told me about him, he should be in the front row two nights from now."

"I suppose so."

"That's when we'll take care of him."

"I hope so," she said. "Right now, I'm going to go over my song list for the performance."

"Okay," Clint said. "While you do that, I'm going downstairs and see if the dining room is a likely place for us to have supper. I'll check back with you, later. Do you still have the gun I gave you?"

"I do."

"Then lock the door behind me."

He stepped into the hall and waited to hear the lock, then headed for the lobby.

***

In order to be sure about the dining room, he had to take a look at the kitchen. He put forth his request to the desk clerk, who said, "Sure, Mr. Adams. Come on, I'll take you back there, right now."

As they walked, the clerk said, "We got some of the best dishes in town. Especially the steak."

"That sounds good."

"Did you and the lady find someplace to eat this afternoon?" he asked.

"The Mayflower."

"Still a good one," the clerk said. "A lot of the other places in town have gone straight downhill."

"That's too bad."

"The whole town's dyin'," the clerk said. "I give it ten more years."

"Then where will you go?"

"Who knows?" the clerk said. "But I'll find someplace. Come, let's look at the kitchen."

The clerk led Clint through the dining room to the kitchen, where a man and a woman were cooking.

"Why are you in my kitchen?" the woman demanded. She was about fifty, and very hard looking. The man seemed about ten years younger, and Clint would have bet he was afraid of her.

"Helga," the clerk said, "Mr. Adams wanted to see if he should eat dinner here, or go elsewhere."

"Here, of course," she said. "My kitchen is the best in Tombstone."

"Better than the Mayflower?" Clint asked.

"You ate at the Mayflower?" she asked.

"This afternoon."

"If you eat here tonight, you will not be disappointed," she told him.

"Can you give him something to taste?" the clerk asked.

"No," she said. "He will have to take my word for it, until tonight."

"The chanteuse from the East, Miss Clarice DuPont, will be eating with him."

The woman's eyebrows went up.

"I have a ticket for her performance."

"Then she'll experience your performance tonight," Clint said, "and you'll experience her in two nights."

The cook put her hands on her ample hips and said to Clint, "She will not be disappointed. I hope I will not, either."

"You won't."

"Then I will see you both tonight for dinner. Come down around eight."

"We'll be here," Clint said. "Thank you."

She glared at the desk clerk.

"Now get out of my kitchen."

Chapter Forty-Two

Clint brought Clarice down to the dining room at eight o'clock. He was surprised to find it empty. All tables had been moved to the side but for one, which was set in the center of the room.

"Just for us?" Clarice asked. "I'm impressed."

"I told you, she has a ticket for your performance. She wants to impress you."

"Then let's see if she can," Clarice said.

A waiter approached them and said, "This way, please."

He seated them at their table, spread napkins on their laps.

"Tonight we're serving wild turkey in plum sauce," he said. "Sure isn't somethin' Tombstone is used to seein', but our cook likes to experiment."

"Sounds good," Clarice said. "Tell your cook I'm looking forward to it."

"I will," the waiter said. "The first course is tomato soup."

"Can't wait," Clarice said.

As the waiter went to the kitchen, Clarice looked at Clint and said, "This is certainly not what I expected from Tombstone."

The soup came out first, and then the wild turkey, soaked in plum sauce and surrounded by vegetables. Clint and Clarice dug in and both were very impressed. When they completed their meal and the waiter removed the plates, Helga, the cook, came out.

"How was your meal?" she asked.

"It was wonderful," Clarice said. "You are the cook?"

"I am," the woman said. "I am Helga."

"I understand you have a ticket for my performance at the Birdcage."

"I do."

"I only hope I impress you as much as you impressed me tonight."

"Thank you," Helga said. "Dessert?"

"Something simple would be nice," Clint said. "Peach pie and coffee?"

"Coming up," she said, and returned to the kitchen. In moments the waiter appeared with the pie and coffee.

"Enjoy."

"They sure have laid out a welcome for us," Clarice said. "I wonder if the Birdcage will do the same?"

"We'll find that out tomorrow. For now, let's finish eating and go to our rooms."

"Are you forgetting something?" she asked.

"What's that?"

"I told you I needed you tonight."

"No, I haven't forgotten."

"Good," she said, "because it still goes."

Clint smiled and said, "Then maybe we should get to it—I mean, if it will relax you."

Clarice smiled.

***

When they got into Clarice's room she turned to Clint and came into his arms. Their kiss went on for some time. When they came up for air Clarice said, "Oh, I've missed this."

"It was a good idea to keep our relationship businesslike for most of the tour," Clint said.

"Until now," she said.

She backed away from him, reached behind her to undo her dress, and dropped it to the floor. Apparently, she had planned for this, as she was now completely naked. She came to him again and pressed her naked body to him. He lifted her in his arms and carried her to the bed. For the next few hours, they thought of nothing but each other. Not the Birdcage Theater, not Clarice's performances, and certainly not the glaring man . . .

***

Clint and Clarice slept in her room that night. In the morning, pleasantly fatigued from a full night of love-making, they dressed and had breakfast together in the dining room.

Afterward, they were able to walk from their hotel to the Birdcage to meet with the musicians.

The Birdcage was not open for business yet, so there was no one in the bar, and no one in the whore's cribs. Clint and Clarice were able to enter through the front door and make their way to the theater. There they encountered several of the musicians tuning and cleaning their instruments.

"I'm Clint Adams," he said, "and this is Clarice DuPont."

"The chanteuse from the East," one of the men said. "A pleasure."

"Where is your bandleader?" she asked. "I need to go over my songs with him."

"Well," the musician said, "we don't really have a band leader."

"What?" she blurted. "Then who . . ."

"We put this band together ourselves, and every night one of us runs it. When we heard about you, we agreed to book you into the Birdcage."

"Then who do I go over my songs with?" she asked.

"Well, it was kind of my idea to book you in here, so I guess for this performance, that'd be me. My name's Yancy Folkes. Just call me Yancy."

"Where can we go over my songs?" she asked.

"Well," Yancy said, "right here. These fellas are Chip and Doug. The other boys will be here tonight, and we'll rehearse with them. But don't you worry. By tomorrow night we'll be ready."

Clarice looked at Clint.

"You've been in the Birdcage before, Mr. Adams," Yancy said. "When the Earps were here. You know we can do it."

"I'd say you don't have a choice, Clarice," Clint said. "These are your boys."

"Shall we go over the songs, Ma'am?" Yancy asked.

"I suppose so," she said.

"I'll wait outside," Clint said. "Then we'll walk back to the hotel."

"Right this way, Ma'am," Yancy said.

Clarice followed him, and Clint left the theater. The three men waiting for him outside drew their guns.

Chapter Forty-Three

As Clint stepped out the front door of the Birdcage, he saw the three men spread out on the street in front of him. All were wearing holstered pistols. The street and boardwalks around the building were empty, so people already knew something was happening.

"I don't suppose we need to introduce ourselves," Clint said.

"You're Adams, the Gunsmith," one of them said.

"Who we are don't matter," the second one said.

"What we're here to do does matter," the third one said.

"And that is?" Clint asked.

"To put you in the ground," the first one said.

"Okay, then," Clint said. "If we're going to do this, let's get it done. I've got more important business."

"You sound real sure of yourself, Adams," the third man said.

"Well," Clint said, "I've done this many, many times before, and I'm still standing. What do you think that means?"

"Shut up!" the first man yelled. "Everybody just shut up and let's do this!"

"I agree," Clint said.

All three men were very nervous. They were probably being paid to do this, but you can't pay anyone to be confident.

Clint decided to stop talking, and just wait. When facing more than one man it was always wise to try and take out the fastest one first. However, this was a situation where Clint didn't know these men, so he didn't know who was the fastest. He was going to have to make a judgment call. He decided the man in the center was calling the shots. He would take him out, first. His peripheral vision was good enough to watch all three men, but he concentrated hardest on the man in the middle, figuring he would make the first move.

When the man made his move Clint drew and fired. His bullet struck the man dead center and he fell to the ground, landing on his gun.

When facing more than one man he never stood still. He fired, and then he moved. Clint ducked left and fired again, killing a second man. The third man acted fast and threw his hands in the air.

"D-don't shoot!" he cried.

"Take your gun out slow and toss it," Clint ordered.

The man did as he was told, tossing the gun away.

"Now," Clint said, approaching him, "we're going to have a talk."

Chapter Forty-Four

Clint questioned the third man, then turned him over to the local marshal, a man named Tim Locane. When he explained the situation, Locane was happy to cooperate.

The gunman, a man named Dalton, told Clint he had been hired by a man he had never met before. When Clint described the glaring man, Dalton confirmed that was the man who had hired him and the other two. He wanted Clint Adams killed on this day, and didn't care how. The three men decided they would be able to outdraw a Gunsmith they considered to be overrated. Sadly, they were mistaken.

When Clarice came out, the bodies had been removed and Clint was able to keep the incident from her. They went back to the hotel and she spent the day resting her voice.

Clint spent the day figuring out what to do about the glaring man.

***

Clint figured the glaring man would have to make a move during Clarice's final performance, if he intended to do anything beyond just glaring at her. In the past she had said she continuously saw him in the front row. Since his three hired guns had failed to kill Clint, he doubted that would be the case tonight. The Birdcage Theater had raised boxes, and one of those would be ideal. But the question was, what was the glaring man's end game?

He walked Clarice to the edge of the stage, where she would enter from.

"This is my last performance," she said. "He's going to try something, otherwise what was the point."

"I want you to keep your eye on those boxes," Clint said.

"But he'll be in the first row," she said.

"Not tonight, he won't," Clint said.

"What can he do from up there?" she asked.

"If all he wants to do is glare at you, he can do that from anywhere," Clint said.

"But if he wants to kill me, he can do it from up there."

"Right. He'd have a clear shot."

"Couldn't he do it better from the first row?"

"It would be easier for him to get away from up there," Clint said.

"But you won't let him, will you?" she asked.

"No, I won't."

"And now," Yancy called from the stage, "the Chanteuse from the East, Miss Clarice DuPont."

"Are you sure?" Clarice asked Clint.

"I'm sure."

All the boxes had a clear view of the stage, But Clint also had a clear view of all the boxes *from* the stage. And so did Clarice.

Clarice started her first song and Clint had heard enough of her performances that he could sense the tension in her tone. He could even see her searching the audience for the glaring man.

Clint had no idea what weapon, if any, the man would use. His only clue was the way Leo Delaware had been killed in New York. But that was done close up. There was no way the man was going to get that close to Clarice. And a box seat would not be close enough to throw a knife, so the only alternative would be a gun.

By Clarice's third song her tone had smoothed out, but Clint could see she was still searching the audience. He was keeping his eyes on the boxes. They all appeared to be occupied by patrons enjoying the show.

Then, as Clarice started her final song, Clint noticed something odd. One of the boxes seemed to have emptied, indicating someone had left before the end of the show. He searched his memory, and realized a man and a woman had been in that box. Now they were gone.

He drew his gun and waited. As Clarice was ending her last song, he saw the barrel of a gun poke out of the box, aimed at the stage. He quickly fired three shots into the box. The barrel disappeared. Several ladies screamed, and Clarice rushed off stage.

"Stay here!" he shouted.

He ran from the stage to the hallway behind the boxes. Number two was the one he wanted. He burst through the door with his gun still in his hand. On the floor in one corner, a man and a woman were trussed up tightly, and gagged. In the front of the box a man was lying on the floor. Clint leaned down and turned the man over. His face was twisted in pain, but he was alive. Two of Clint's three shots had hit him. There was a gun on the floor next to him. Clint kicked it away, then turned to the trussed up couple and untied them.

"He burst into the box with his gun out and tied us up," the man said.

"Are you both all right?"

"I think so, Dear?"

"I'm fine," she said, then looked at Clint. "Thank you so much."

At that moment Clarice burst into the box. On the floor the audience was rushing out.

"Clint!"

“Is that him, Clarice?” Clint asked, pointing. “Is that your glaring man?”

Clarice looked at the man and said, “That’s him.”

The man looked up at Clarice. “Nora!” He said, and then fell unconscious.

“He needs a doctor,” Clint said.

“Well, you’re in luck,” the man lying next to his wife said. “I’m a doctor.”

***

When Clarice unlocked the door to her room Clint stepped inside and closed it.

“Is he alive?”

“He is,” Clint said, “and he’s in jail.”

“Did you identify him?”

“He had papers on him identifying him as someone named Francis Winchester.”

“Oh my,” she said. “Of the Boston Winchesters?”

“Apparently.”

“Why would a member of one of Boston’s richest families behave in such a way?”

“Let’s have a seat,” Clint said, “and a drink.”

He held up a bottle of wine for her to see.

“There are two glasses here,” she said.

She sat on the sofa—the only room in the hotel with such a comfort—while Clint poured two glasses, and then joined her.

"Did he say anything to explain himself?"

"Apparently, he thinks you're a lady he knew named Nora," Clint said. "She spurned his advances."

"Why would he think I was her?" she asked. "Why wouldn't he just go after her?"

"Well, it seems he killed her," Clint said, "but then saw you and thought he'd missed. He decided to follow you all the way to Tombstone before trying again."

"How did he know my schedule?"

"He had it in his pocket," Clint said. "He must have gotten it when he killed your manager, Delaware."

"He must be mad!" she said.

"Oh, he is," Clint said. "He's bat shit crazy."

"But he's in custody now," she said.

"Oh yes," Clint said. "The marshal is going to ship him back to Boston to stand trial. But I have a question for you."

"What's that?"

"Why did Delaware book you into Abilene and Denver, and then Tombstone? It would have made more sense for him to have sent you from St. Louis, down the Mississippi to New Orleans, and then to Tombstone."

"Oh," she said, "Leo hated New Orleans. You see, he grew up there, and it was not a happy childhood.

"Well, I'd suggest the next time you tour you include it," Clint said. "They would love you there. And their theaters are quite beautiful. And the food—"

"I'll make a deal with you," she said. "I'll play New Orleans if you take me there."

They clinked glasses and he said, "You have a deal."

Upcoming New Release!

THE GUNSMITH

BELLE STARR'S DAUGHTER
BOOK 483

Belle Starr's daughter, Rosie Lee Reed, barely twenty, runs a large bordello and saloon in a town in Alabama. She is attacked on the street and Clint is there to protect her. After that she asks Clint if he will help her resist attempts to take over her business…

For more information
visit: www.SpeakingVolumes.us

Now Available!

THE GUNSMITH

BOOKS 430 – 481

For more information

visit: www.SpeakingVolumes.us